Martin (Murt) Malone, Máirtín Ó Maoileoin authored the award-winning novel *Us*, a book shortlisted for the Irish Novel of the Year Award and winner of The Sunday Independent/Dr John B Keane Literature Bursary. *The Broken Cedar* was nominated for an IMPAC Award, and optioned for screen, as was *After Kafra*. He has won RTÉ's Francis MacManus Award and An Cuirt Literary Prize for his short story *The Mango War*, and was nominated for The Sunday Times EFG Short Story Prize with *Valley of the Peacock Angel* and commissioned by the National Art Gallery of Ireland to write for *Lines of Vision, Irish Writers on Art*. BBC Radio 4 produced *Dream Horse*, along with several other stories, while RTE Drama produced three of his radio plays. Moat Theatre Group brought *Rosanna Nightwalker, the Wren of the Curragh* to stage.

"In art it is hard to say anything as good as saying nothing."
Wittgenstein

First published in 2026
Owl Fella's Press
Moat View
Kilmead, Athy
Co. Kildare R14YN92

Cover design by
Valerie Ó Maoileoin

Layout by April Sky Design, Newtownards

ISBN: 978-1-0369-2461-4

We gratefully acknowledge the assistance of Kildare County Arts Service.

Pike Hill

The Rath Massacre

A Novel

Martin Malone

Pike Hill, aka The Long Hill, Gibbet Rath

The Memory of the Dead

(Who Fears to Speak of '98)

Who fears to speak of Ninety-Eight?
Who blushes at the name?
When cowards mock the patriot's fate,
Who hangs his head for shame?
He's all a knave or half a slave,
Who slights his country thus,
But a true man, like you man,
Will fill your glass with us.

JOHN KELLS INGRAM

In memory of Seoirse Ó Maoileoin and his 1798 comrades from St Mullins, who fell at the battle for New Ross on 5th June 1798, and to those massacred at Gibbet Rath on the Curragh Plains Tuesday 29th May while present to complete terms of surrender.

In war, while killing others, we are also killing ourselves.

Limited edition

(70, author initialled)

Prologue

Tuesday 29 May 1798
Eventide

Nervously, a chain of prospective widows and orphans begin to ascend the long sloping hill from town, toward grassland patched with purpled tipped thistle and yellow furze – their destination crests at the large rath, ancestral home of a clan refugeed by Normans to the Wicklow mountains. A chain of frightened souls, stomachs bitterly soured from what might await them – concerning those who have not come home, because they are either dead or on the run or held captive. A cauldron of unknown and worrying currents.

Evening is closing in, the air cooling by degrees. Blue skies and sun are not as refulgent as at the start of the day, when no one dreamed of a bad ending such as had occurred. Crows raucously sound-off; a magpie perches on the limb of a lone hawthorn in white bloom; green ribbons dangle from other branches; wishes – a cursed tree some say – a species to be left alone. A May tree. Haunt of things not of this world: the little people, the banshee, the Wizard Earl, the ghosts of Lughnasa. Pookas. Prayerful whispers to entities perhaps kinder than God and less cruel than Satan.

Elizabeth pauses to draw her breath. Perspiration stings her eyes, her pale face toasted red from the days of broiling heat. Blinks and brings her knuckles to her right eye, smaller than her other, more prone to suffering rheumy bouts; eyes of differing colours: brown, green.

For moments she studies the eastern skies. There are beautiful mountains to the east and backdrops of ridged peaks behind them, and more behind these, showing shades of fading ink. Twilight veiling the day.

Against this…in the lowering of her eyes.

Buttercups and furzy petals are freckled with blood on the approach to a dirt track that winds like a river with many bends. Leads out to acres strewn with bodies, of green flags and pennants patterned with yellow harps, of cockades discarded as the rebels fled. The air reeks from the ash of smouldering campfires, spilled blood, human entrails and severed limbs, slaughtered horses. There are piles of bodies, too…heaped as a cairn, wantonly.

Silent and whispering utterances of prayer to the Mother of Christ cease in the rush to determine the fate of a husband or a son, and to catch news of sisters made captive for sole purpose. Grief rises above stricken awe, tones of harrowing grief, of disbelief oust the air of prayer.

Whilst scavenging birds flutter at the cries from distraught and angered women and children, flies hover around the remains, seeking moments in the goriest of repast.

Bodies are turned to ascertain their identities. Facial features do not always satisfy the unspoken question; the map of the fallen severely disfigured. When identified as loved ones, the wailing dashes to higher octaves and further develops as evening light continues its descent. Though far from silent now, when the silence arrives it will be remembered as having sounded loudest.

The work of discovery continues; there are late arrivals and the reappearing of carts to ferry more remains to bury in hollowed tombs cut from sun hardened earth.

The sky darkens and perforations of starlight and a strip of moon feature, an occasional drifting cloud. And the shrieking of banshee widows and fatherless children lessens, cooled by the falling dew, the doing of the grim necessary; primeval instinct instils a temporary stitching of shock and numbness to allow the recognizing, the ugly wounds, the lifting of corpses on to the blood-soaked cars.

In the dawn mist, down the long hill, carts convey the dead and those near death to graves yet to be carved. Town gravediggers too need burying…

Chorusing the gloomy and slow-moving caravan are muttered prayers, sessions of weeping, the neighing of a horse, a donkey's braying, the lurching of wheels on rutted ground, the tangible sense of severe loss, not only of life but that of freedom, and hope. Gone now, the eyes of the dead see nothing – the living are blind too. But the fireside seanchaí would say in days to come, that hope never really dies. It is only ever put to rest for a time; a rebel heart with just cause never loses its beat. He would say for now we take solaces from wherever we can find them.

The week before…

A breeze of risen hurts blows across this neck of the plains, the grasslands rippling as agitated sea waters. Gilded medallions quiver on gorse in full bloom, spiny thorns topped with deceitful smiles. The mountains to the east field flanks of purple heather as war shields.

He turns his grey horse from the scene, the breeze behind him and his group of men, heading towards town, to the plumes of smoke rising above the round tower in the cathedral grounds. Brigid's place. Her kitchen, her extinguished fire, where her final breath crossed the bridge of life.

Dennis blesses himself slowly, as though pushing a burden up and down a steep hill.

He considers whether there's any good in a breeze that isn't cooling on the hottest of days.

*

Louise watches with a child's feline curiosity the red coated militia traipse from the town's market square. Concern agitates her, shows in a deep frown. She leans her back against the well's stone parapet, its stones shaded by the market square building are cool against her lower spine. Cavalry horses dance on the edge of their hooves, flanks foamed from nervousness and a torturing sun. The stepping of hooves creates small clouds of tanned dust. A horse's ears shivers like a river weed caught in a breeze. Pennants hang low as chastened heads, alarmed voices rise high, adding another ingredient; that of a heightening danger. A bay horse bucks and whinnies, is brought under control by language of a colour new to Louise's ears. Enough now, she thinks, growing fearful, the edge of excitement and curiosity blunted.

There are few people around to see them off; people fled in a hurry on hearing the new thunder, witnessing the starker lightning, sensing the change of mood, the widening width of differences between the townspeople, the hard stare, sullen quietness, the broodiness. Smiles veneered inner feelings, truth revealed by the eyes, the averted look.

The militia are leaving for the county town of Naas, 15 miles distant, to await further orders, so the captain had earlier told Grandfather. News of insurgent victories in other towns close-by had excited the local community and alarmed certain individuals. Including Nana, who doesn't require much to worry her; she frets and fusses continually, so much so she has a harried look to her. Sometimes, Louise thinks, Nana's worries bring her to a point where she forgets her manners; more than once Louise had walked into the drawing room to catch her picking her nose, oblivious to what she was doing. Staring through the window at her mind's far-off things. Perhaps on the dreams her life had never harvested.

Louise sees a straggle of people emerge from the narrow streets connected to the square, noticeably from Firecastle Lane that runs alongside the curtain wall of the cathedral and its broken toothed round tower. It is as though they had been in waiting for the militia to withdraw. She looks at the crenelations of the cathedral, the round tower – yesterday she had played hide-go-seek with

Sally in the grounds and ventured down the rough steps into Saint Brigid's kitchen to hide in its darkest corner, ignoring Sally's calls to show herself. Her anxious appeals became increasingly shriller the longer she delayed. Poor Sally.

The square begins to fill as an incoming tide of people.

A snub-nosed man discharges a musket, startling her into drawing her hands to her face. Loud cries and shouts as the square masses; some break away and force their way into Sanderson's Inn. The Sandersons had left for Naas ahead of the militia, flushed red as the militia's jackets. With the sound of breaking glass in her ears, she turns and hurries across the road. Runs as hard as she can ever remember running, the air scalding her lungs, a pain biting at her side. Her long fair hair carries behind her, almost as a pennant. Her oval face is pale, and she has little craters above her eyebrow where she had picked at chickenpox scabs. 12 years old.

Veering left, gravel rustles under her feet along the avenue, she increases her pace past the medieval Fitzgerald tower house, toward the blue double doors, open wide to allow cool air to enter the house. Trellises of red roses flank the doorway, recently watered before the sun had heightened, and are now in the shaded heart of the day, wilting despite their morning shower. Breathless, her hand pressed to her side, she pants into the hallway,

"Grandfather, come quickly."

He calls to her from behind, "Louise?"

She turns, fighting to catch her breath, "The militia have left town…and there are people in the square, lots of people. They have broken into Sanderson's Inn."

George looks at his granddaughter and then at his wife who had come from the kitchen. Nellie wears a disturbed look. Concern about everything and anything shows easily on her features. Worries about things that will never happen, or what people think of her, a hair out of a place, a look from a body misconstrued as wayward – no matter that the ratio of her worries and suspicions is 1 in a 100 times accurate, the 1 is sufficient for her to justify her reasoning for "…always keeping an eye on things."

She wearies him daily. Louise thinks Father is right, her tongue would wear a turtle's carapace to dust, she so forgets to let up.

A small woman and lightly built, with heavily engraved lines across her forehead, and a deep niche between eyebrows where some troubles had fallen farthest.

Nellie says, "We should go with them, George. I told you – the captain advised too…we should-."

He reflects for moments before saying with a confidence he did not feel, "Divil a bit. No, no, we'll be fine, dear, prepare something for us to eat. Louise, good girl, will you go draw all the curtains and pull over the storm shutters. Ask Hannah to help you."

"Hannah's gone,' Nellie says darkly, "she left us early."

They watch the child skip down the hallway.

Nellie says, "George…just because you can't see the devil's horns, it doesn't follow that they're not there."

"Shush, Nellie. We'll not come to any harm. Don't we employ Hannah – her brother is a leader with them. I'm not in the militia anymore – what would they want with old folk like us. Nellie, eh? Hannah will tell them that we are not to be harmed. We've been decent to her. Have we not?"

Nellie says quietly, "She upped and left without saying a word kind."

George touches his weak chin, "She's usually full of goodbyes."

He goes to speak but while his lips move, they pour no words. He has not been well this past while and his thoughts have become slow to mature and there are bouts of forgetfulness that irritate Nellie and mystify himself.

"Which is why, George, I say that we must make our way to Naas this instant. Now is not the time to be dally."

Silence. Broken by successive discharges of musket, not close. There's the rising hue and cry of the crowd. If he can hear them, with his hearing, they are too close. Of the news that had chased Louise home…yes. But. Yet he sees no reason to harbour any serious trepidation: after all they are on speaking terms with their catholic neighbours, contribute regularly to the poor box, had never turned away a hungry mouth.

We're not the Sandersons.

But there is something in the summer air that in all his 76 years he had not experienced. It is as though the scorched earth is yielding up centuries of injustices, extracted by the fierce heat from a sun that appears fused with Midas's touch on the islands of furze on the nearby plains. Or a poultice, perhaps: drawing the badness out of the earth. Infecting the citizenry into doing themselves and everyone else some terrible harms.

"George, please. Stop with one of your trances."

"Okay. You could be right, my dear – perhaps it would be wise to leave."

Nellie sighs relief and says, "I'll go and pack a few things for the journey. Will you ready the car?"

"Aye, I would if its wheel was sound,' he says, only now remembering its brokenness.

Nellie says, "Jay, I forgot. The horses so. We may leave our things behind."

George whispers consent.

Wringing her thickly veined hands she says, "We should hurry. We should have hurried yesterday."

George says, galvanising himself, "Louise is slight – she can ride with me. You take the brown lad."

*

The depth of the quietness strikes Louise on the landing. Eerie, she thinks. This stillness. Worse than the Curragh winds howling into town, stirring the beams in the attic, creaks and moans, rattling doors and windows in their frames. Draughts sharp as blades to her very marrow. Stealing in even on a fine sunny day, in a mild breeze from the Gibbet Rath where Grandfather said the fairies and pookas still lived and came out at night to dance around the corpse of a hanged highwayman. Whistled along the Race of the Black Pig, the trail Grandfather said was used by Fionn MacCumhail and his warriors, and by the Wizard Earl who rode his silver shod horse along it once a year. Oh, but none of his stories has ever been as chilling as this silence. If she were here Sally would be roaring her eyes out with the fright. Or struck dumb. She wonders at her friend's whereabouts and why she hadn't called for her to come out and play like she had done every day so far this summer. Suddenly, Nana calling her name pierces her thoughts.

*

In her small front yard, standing beside a yew tree, Elizabeth hears the commotion bellowing from the square. Raucous behaviour emanates from blind drunk patriots celebrating the town's so-called liberation. Her home lies at the end of a downhill road from town, a decent sized dwelling with outhouses and an oblong orchard of crab apple trees. The sun has fallen, leaving in its wake a reddish glow that reminds her of a scene in a painting hung on the wall of a manor house where she used to work as a maid. A beautiful serenity shows in the Franciscan ruins adjacent their land; the abbey lapsed into dereliction after King Henry's men at arms had evicted them. Centuries ago. She remembers Dennis saying royalties are interred in the graveyard, Fitzgeralds notably. Who cares, she'd thought. Curbing her tongue not to add why he sounded almost genuflective, he who detested the blue bloods... who believe we should do as the French did almost a decade ago. You'd want the power of ten tongues to drill sense into Dennis's head.

Dennis is home but reluctantly so, the eejit of a man. If common sense fell as rain, he would never get wet. She can almost feel the itch in him to be away again, to climb on his horse and re-join his comrades. He'd arrived an hour ago to let her know he was fine, had survived the battles and skirmishes at Prosperous and Clane. *To let you know...* I can see, she'd responded, what's in front of me.

Rumours of what had happened in those villages had reached her and she hadn't liked hearing of the death toll according to Bridie Flanagan. She is a woman given to exaggeration and Elizabeth hopes she is true to her form. Folly, the lot of it, she thinks, though she understands that people had been severely provoked. Pitching and tarring of suspected United Irishmen by Prosperous militia had incensed the likes of Dennis. Tell the truth, men like Dennis keep gardens of justifications to give themselves reasons to react but never maintain a garden for why they should not forsake their place; the chief one is the flower of not doing anything to make matters worse than they are already.

Her husband had regaled her with tales of cavalry and pike charges, how they'd put militia and yeomanry to flight. Such excitement in his brown eyes. And then he set to taking her with a passion she thought had been long spent between them. She'd responded eagerly, crying out with pleasure in their bed chamber, forgetting herself in the moments of ecstasy, just catching herself in time and biting on the pillow before a loud moan left her – their two young children might have come in from the fields with their grandfather. It would be shameful for them to hear the rocking of the bed, the grunts and groans, their parents simultaneous release. Shameful because she believed it best not to tease people's senses, to make them curious, to stir them into looking at you in a new light. There was an order of things to be maintained. Etiquette. Shameful also because it was fear, excitement, and death that had watered Dennis's senses; in a peculiar way had given him a new life.

The loudness of the victory celebration ascends in a flurry of beating drums. Whoops and wails of joy. A storm smiling on a bright sunny day.

"Where are the childer?" he asks, dressed now, fixing his trousers, tightening his leather belt to its latest speared eyelet.

They are walking past the trellis of roses to his grey stallion, tethered to a wooden pole.

"The field…I don't know," she says, "I hope they're not up there with that lot. They're burning people out of their homes, Dennis – our neighbours."

"Only a couple, them as belonging to the yeomanry. They were never our neighbours, not in the right sense of the meaning."

His horse whinnies and shifts on its hooves. He pats her flank and says "Settle!"

Elizabeth looks in the direction of the voluminous clouds of smoke, her nose crinkling.

"It's like piss burning, that thatch and slate," he says for her.

A close enough description, she thinks.

"Won't you come with me?" he says, "for a while?"

He is a tall man, well-built with a ruddy complexion, turning paunchy, blond bull's wool hair. While she is slightly structured, black-haired, and pretty enough to have drawn much better looking than her husband. She had fallen for his quiet humour, his easy way, his lack of interest in ale, and of course his means. He has changed though. His humour had died off, he'd taken to drinking, his fortune (comparatively speaking to those of their class) is now almost depleted. All that remains of the man she had married 14 years ago is his easy way, though aspects of this have changed too – he is too easily swayed. Enchanted by bull talk, something her father had said of him having "…a looseness to his thought."

"You ask, Dennis, but I sense that in the heel of the hunt you really don't want me there with you…I would be a distraction… you would fear me saying the wrong thing. So. I will not," she says, 'and you should not be going there either."

Take control of this man.

"Elizabeth…I watched the Ancient Hibernians shoot two of my first cousins and hang another and they were innocent men. You know this. You above all should understand that I can't sit at home and do nothing – I'm not. I can't. I won't."

"This is all going to end badly, don't you see that? You must. You're not a fool."

"I believe we have a chance of succeeding…I'm an officer and-"

"Stop with that oul blather, Dennis. You're a farmer. An officer, you are not."

"Indeed,' he says, his features gradually hardening, "I was never much in your eyes to begin with."

She casts that remark aside with a quick shake of her head and says, "You're risking everything – and you've got more to lose than very many of the others. They're risking nothing in comparison."

He reaches out to caress her hair but she shies away. He says, "Do you think that their lives are nothing?"

"You know well what I mean. They have no property to lose. You'll…we'll lose our farm, our start on them."

"We are losing what little we own bit by bit – selling a plot of land here to pay for this and that. Struggling to put food on the table – there's not much difference between having little and nothing and people like me – we're bloody fed up with trying to balance that sort of life."

"So, we'll all be rich when the rebellion is done?"

"The English and their lackeys have no business being here, they never had."

Not having an answer to her question, he'd deviated.

"The people you're fighting are nearly all Irish," she says.

"Come along for the craic. Meet my men. There are women with whom you can work."

"Your men? The craic. I am quite certain there are women."

Oh, Jaysus save us.

"Those men are under my command. You might not but others see something better than average qualities in me. Some of their women are helping out with the cooking, even with the fighting."

"I can well imagine their sort. Dennis Downey. You're next to a moron. You haven't paid the least notice to my advice. You'll go to Naas, Dennis? For the protection notice, won't you?"

He shakes his head; suggestive of her being impossible.

"No, far from it," he says.

A flame stirs in her, stoked by the innate portend of an approaching maelstrom.

"You cannot be serious. You're not staying involved in this madness. The ructions in the town. Listen to it. Does that sound like an army to you?"

"What do you want of me – I'm not a coward, and…"

"Want of you? Do you really need telling, merciful God. Are you Jaspar Dunny I'm talking to?"

"I'm no fool, watch your mouth."

"You'd want to start thinking more of me and Sally and Jack and less about your bleddy Roger McGarry. When are you are going to start thinking about us in all of this?"

You'd think by his pout that I'd just insulted the Pope.

"Elizabeth-".

"No, you listen! You get that notice before the tide turns because that's all will prevent us from being burned out of it when the militias return – and return they will."

Silence.

She continues, "Mark my words."

His response is uttered quietly but forcibly, "You'd have me ride to Naas and throw myself at the mercy of that crowd. What if one of them pipes up that he'd seen me in action – I'd be strung up on the spot. That's as sure as the sun rises. Because it happened this morning to Billy Harris who heeded his gobshite wife's utterings and tarried off with himself along to Naas."

"Oh," she says, the news catching in her throat.

"Dennis," she pleads.

He sighs long and hard, chews on his lower lip, eyeing her as though he scarcely recognises her.

"Have you killed?" she asks, "is that what you can't bring yourself to tell me?"

He has gone from her, walking, his horse behind him, its head lowered, mimicking Dennis.

*

For God's sake – let the man speak! the barrel-chested man roars, the sun blazing on the blunderbuss's flared muzzle prior to his squeezing the trigger.

Roger McGarry does not know the shooter beyond his name, Boots Tiernan. He steps forward of Tiernan to the edge of the dray. He feels hot and sticky. Nettle rash on his forearms, gained from throwing himself onto the ground when shot at in Clane, stings through the balm of dock leaf. The crowd quietens by degrees. He knows he will never gain complete silence. In front of him stand perhaps 2000 men and women and children – many armed with whatever weapon they imagined could serve as one, wearing green cockades and sashes embroidered with a yellow harp. Pikes, muskets, flintlocks, swords, not nearly enough of any, he thinks. A crucial lack of cannon; 1 Three-pounder and 2 Six-pounders; 13 rounds of ammunition among them. Not a sinner here with experience in firing them. Distance will do for us, narrowing it whenever suits us to enable effective use of the pike – it comes down to measurements – any fool knows that if you can kill your enemy at a maximum range of 80 yards, and he can kill you from a range of 120 yards…the conclusion sounds as a banshee shriek. Ring out the mourning bell for the rebel dead.

Liquor looted from the burning tavern opposite the square's market building has put the crowd in a boisterous and dangerous mood – ready to turn, ready to take things into their own hands, ready to deafen themselves against reason.

Of stocky build, balding, thick sideburns, he has unexpectedly found himself at the head of the rebels and isn't too sure if he likes the command status entrusted upon him by the death of Squire Merrigan, who'd taken a sabre slash to his throat during a skirmish yesterday. 22 militia deaths in Naas, 50 in Prosperous, against seven losses at the latter battle for his own tiny and ill-equipped force. Though overall they had lost 203 men. Surprise, ferocity, and persistence had been effective. But surprise will not always work; the bravest and most ferocious among them had been the first to die in battle and for many of the others persistence lasted for as long as alcohol stewed in their veins.

Not much by way of cavalrymen either. We need those too. *Christ, is there anything we don't bleddy need?*

Where the hell is Fitzgerald? he thinks. The other leaders? *I should be a back figure on this stage. Have they been captured?* This is highly possible. McGarry was quick to grasp the fact that there wasn't a trained military man on the volunteers' committee, and this did not augur well for future engagements with the enemy. *Still, I cannot show doubt – if they sense it, we have nary a chance at all. Christ, spare us...I feel like a stuck pig.*

He inhales deeply and then roars. "Kildare town is free and there's another place where we are going...are ye with me, boys – For Monasterevin in the morn!"

A town six miles to the west.

Boots Tiernan cups his hand about McGarry's ear and says, "We have a man to dangle from a rope, a bastard yeoman the Foxford Shires left behind."

"Does he know the workings of a cannon?"

"He wouldn't know the workings of his tool."

*

Days before...

Where the Grand Canal affiliates with the river Barrow, McGarry walks the trail with the blacksmith John Sixpence, a portly man with a gimp leg, who fished the waters, whose forge and home were burned to the ground nearly two months ago, and his son tarred and pitched; his scalp and face strawberry coloured and disfigured. Eyesight burned almost to naught.

"I'm living off what fish I catch," Sixpence says, "and the daecency of the Ballitore quakers…and no, Roger, I won't be making any more pikes or joining in a lost cause."

McGarry's eyes turn to the grey heron at the top of a tree, and then there's a sparkle on the waters, a glimpse of a colourful bird flying fast and low above the water, a blur of blue and green.

"Walk with me…my horse is parked at the next bridge."

"Roger, they cleaned us out of weapons in the searches they did a while back – when they suspected something was afoot…we should have risen before then…now it's too late."

"They've dislodged the boulder from the mountain top, like it or not – it's in motion and twill break whatever gets in its way."

"Fitzgerald is no proper leader to be in hiding in Dublin – I heard, did you not, that he has a fancy bottle green uniform ready for the wearing…I don't want to fight for that…for a man and a cause that would spend money on cloth and hat that'd feed a whole village for a week. Jaesus, we'd just be swapping the colour of the dog that's always been biting at us."

McGarry's sigh is like the rasping squeeze of a tired bellows. His eyes catch an arc of a chestnut tree, green on the water, near a canal keeper's thatched house.

"You'll do well, Roger, to take your leave while you can. The end of a rope is all that's waiting there…but if you want that… then I suppose you should go and kill as many of the bastes as God will allow…but no," he beats his chest lightly, "me. I won't shed blood."

"Again, you mean."

"Again."

They slow and then pause a short distance from the stone bridge which crosses to a field where they're once buried arms.

"Are they still there?" McGarry asks.

"They are…how they get out of there is your concern…there are eyes everywhere…the fecks were always good at sniffing us out, even our very thoughts."

"The count."

"About 100 pike heads, a dozen swords – my work is sound. As is Carty's. You-".

"Ah, I know that, John. We were apprenticed to the same smithy; my memories are intact of those days."

"I want nothing for them, so stay your hand on your purse."

"I have the coin to pay you."

"From the United men's purse – miserable curs…not a penny did they give us, no sort of help after the fecking misery hit us."

"Aah, the treasury isn't as flush as you might think, but…"

He presses five sovereigns into the other's hand. Sixsmith stares at them resting on his scarred palm, "If I'm caught with these, they'll swing me, Roger…I couldn't explain their possession."

"Don't get caught, then."

"The river or your pocket, that's down to you," his hand prepared to throw.

McGarry shakes his head in reluctant acceptance.

"Roger, take your leave of what's coming."

The men part at the bridge, and as Roger watches his old friend return along the route they'd walked, a pang of sorrow at his brokenness brings a lump to his throat. He'd never known a man whose spirit was broken beyond salvage. A brave man, a knowledgeable one, his soul charred.

This is what they have done to our people. This is what happens whenever we show our enemies the retaliatory hand. But it is what happens when you steal a man's home, rob him blind, the blood rises. Always. A slow bubble, like a rising blister, it breaks.

This land hereabouts. Ardreigh – it was John who'd told him of the lost village, wiped out by Edward Bruce's men in 1357, the so called Irish High King, on his pillages up and down the east of the country. Fitting that the pikes were buried in the forgotten graveyard, blessed by the proximity of the slaughtered, perhaps. *It's bleddy kings that have brought us nothing only hardship.*

An inner voice encroaches...*only a man with nothing between his ears disregards John Sixpence's advice. His brokenness has earned him wisdom, that of the defeated.*

*

Sickening him, is George's realisation of having left it too late to leave. On the ground floor every window glass appears to simultaneously crash, a shattering of waves against rocks. A fierce wrench sunders the newly painted blue door. The babble and shrieks are terrifying, revealing a spine of utter hatred and a determination to eliminate its source.

Nellie? he thinks. She had gone out back to saddle the horses, saying she would do it quicker than him, thinking of his weak left hand, how arthritis won't permit him to curl his fingers into a fist leave alone a decent grip.

His blunderbuss? Its firing pin is damaged, rendering it useless. A sting of regret punches hard in the pit of his stomach, for putting off its repair, for ignoring his inner voice.

Louise?

In her bedroom.

She'd left Nellie to fetch her doll, a favourite, with the polka dotted dress. In his right hand he carries his old service sword. Unsheathing it, he throws the scabbard on to the bed and walks out onto the landing, then midway down the narrow stairs. Each fall of foot, he experiences a leak of pee, a quake in his knees, a wild wave of dread drowning him.

The intruders do not see him and he wonders if there might still be time to escape, perhaps from an upstairs window on to the roof of the barn? *At my age?* But as he thinks the plan through, they, almost one by one, follow the corner of their eye.

George, his voice shaky but inflamed with anger, shouts, "Out! Out of my home! How dare you!"

They look at him, a little taken aback that he is still here. He keeps his sword behind him to show he is not presenting himself as a threat. A noise of breaking delft carries in from the dining room. A woman's cackle, too.

A red-haired man nearest the foot of the stairs, thin and mean looking with no lower teeth says, "You're not in charge now, bucko. Do ye hear me?"

George does not know this man.

He puts a foot forward and raises his pike, advancing it a reach of 6 feet. George parries its upper shaft with his sword, deflecting the hooked and pointed iron head to pass his side.

The second pike and a third from another he cannot evade. Searing pain in his chest, his throat, his eyes take in the blood spurting from his wounds. Pain. Such pain. Dimly he grows aware of a presence behind him. His eyes scream for her to run.

He hears Louise shout, "Leave my grandfather alone!"

Pike the beggars! A woman says.

"Hannah!" Louise screeches.

*

It's true what his father used to say, Roger thinks 'There's no man with a mannerly streak in him when it comes to feeding his belly and scratching his tool.'

There are things happening by men and women that if done by

their oppressors would be deplored as the worse of injustices to the highest heavens. Flouted under the banner of green and gold harp, of *Erin go Bragh*. Things for which the oppressors will exact a payment stacked with high interest.

He is a man burdened with the weight of a tomb on his shoulders.

And the seed of an idea rises…but taking precedence is to establish, with Boots Tiernan and Downey, outposts at roads leading in and out of town. To have their gains inventoried, organise their food chain, weapons, to train new recruits in the use of a pike – a day's training would suffice; we are in a hurry. To manage the treasury. Tally the count…that which hadn't been plundered and kept hidden by the rabble he leads.

A mob. They are untrained…as we ourselves are, Roger mulls.

Rendezvousing later with Downey and Tiernan at a coach-house on the western outskirts of Kildare, the Monasterevin road, where slip roads merge and run into a crossroads, he says that during night-time checks he found a post abandoned, another guarded by men who were either asleep or drowsy after overly indulging in downing the contents of looted whiskey casks. Dennis Downey reports similar situations elsewhere, gloomily, and then seals his lips, like one would do after receiving the host of Christ at communion – this sealing, however, is caused by a bitter elixir conjured by a travelling apothecarist; there is the stench of reality, too; its hard swallow.

Over tankards of ale Tiernan had brought over to their corner table, he continues "We're waiting on word from whoever's in charge. In the morning we'll take Monasterevin…we have to if we're to keep the momentum going – and by jay do we need to acquire that garrison's arsenal of weapons and gunpowder."

Realities laid bare. A currach without oars will take you nowhere.

Inside the house are wooden chairs, forms lined against dung painted walls, and round tables unsteady on their legs. A counter the length of a coffin, its surface scratched at by coins sliding across it over the years, now owns dark arrowhead veins of long ingrained dirt, shelves hung with a crooked eye are lined with whiskey bottles and others containing mountain dew that touch places in need of special healing. Tobacco pipes channel smoke into emphysemiac lungs which is exhaled as clouded breath – throats hack in an act of clearance, sputum hawked and spat hard onto a sawdust sprinkled floor.

Men breathe ancient thoughts from pools of old thinking patterns, passed down to them like old unwashed rags considered valuable for their holding of sweat, blood and tears, touchstones of the way things once were, love perished, changed ways, intransigent, alike the moonstones and ogham stone that leaned strong from the earth, far outliving the hands who had etched the carvings, the minds that had designed the lunar alignment to shine between the standing stones, onto ritual blood spill.

McGarry has a habit of squinting when listening, as though enlisting the aid of his eyes in the process of hearing. Zeroing as a sharpshooter into what was being said, as though to hear more than the spoken word. To read and define what lay beyond the plains of the tongue; similar to which the hard of hearing do.

"The plan?" Dennis finally says into McGarry's silence.

Tiernan says, "Same as we did with the other towns, I expect."

Dennis reminds them, "The element of surprise is no longer with us. It's going to be difficult to dislodge them – we need to bring them into the open, to create an ambush."

McGarry wets his upper lip with his tongue and then says, "We'll outnumber them.

But as I've said already, we're to receive word – those were my orders at O'Brien's public house in Nurney a week before the rebellion started."

Dennis says, "That's our plan – to simply rush in blindly?"

Tiernan says, "Have you got a better one?"

'Travel lightly, encroach at night, on foot, house to house.'

Tiernan shakes his head and dismisses the idea in a low voice, "That would take an age and a half. Besides, we're not mice that we scurry here and there."

McGarry, sensing a rising tension between the pair, says, "I-"

Dennis says, 'What are we, Boots? Describe us. Old Watson was hanged today – why? You ordered it – the hanging of an 81-year-old. And a drummer boy, too, a mere child.'

Tiernan says, 'The old lad, he – well, 81 – he looked young for his age. The other a cheeky cur he was. He insulted our Brigid, our saints, our priests, our..."

Dennis reaches across and grabs the other's throat. Boots can't believe the suddenness of the action or the strength in Dennis's grip. He is a solid man experienced in stick fighting and wrestling but such a hold he had never experienced. It hurt; he felt his life ebbing. McGarry sits there, saying nothing. Calm, even when he brings his firm hand to Dennis's wrist to lessen the chokehold.

Suddenly, from outside, arrives the screeching sound of coach wheels braking hard on the road, of galloping horses slowing, ninnying. Simultaneous shouts, roars from the duty men. The three men glance at each other and hurry to investigate, Tiernan holding his throat, eyes watering, coughing, croaks, "You and I, Downey, we'll finish things another time."

McGarry forces his way through the crowd, approaching directly the passengers already lined up against the mail-coach. The driver and his companion had been disarmed, and were standing apart from the passengers, as though to indicate these were not their associates and themselves merely hirlings in the course of earning their bread money.

A wiry man says, "One of them's an officer – he said he was a Gifford and that his uncle was a General in Limerick."

"A General no less, is he?"

Pause.

McGarry walks up to the young man. Surmises. A fine-looking lad all right. Tall. Arrogant set to his puss. Typical of his kind with their damned titles and sense of regal superiority.

"What's your name?" he says.

A fellow passenger speaks, "He's an officer."

"Is that true, lad?"

"I'm Lieutenant Michael Gifford – I'm on my way to Limerick, to join up with Major General James Duff, my uncle."

Foolish boyo, McGarry thinks, waving his uncle's name as though for it to carry a threat. In the hope it would garner for him respect and safe passage. A right class of eejit, for certain.

"Join up?" McGarry says, "so you can march against us?"

Realising his gaffe charted lines of apprehension on the young officer's face.

"No. I don't know. How could it be…I heard no word about this on goings."

McGarry recognises the lie – *he didn't know, my foot.* The boy had sensed adventure. Rushed headlong for it without pausing to gather his wits. *Well, now.*

Over his shoulder he says, "Take the others away, let them go…"

He waits for the passengers to be led away before speaking to the officer, "You didn't think we'd have manned the roads – yous came off a by-road…and here we are doing the right thing and here you are for doing the wrong thing."

My own fella is almost as old as him. And I can smell the nerves off this boy.

Standing to the side of the young man, he announces, "What am I to do with this bucko?"

Tiernan snaps, "Hang him."

Dennis intervenes, joining McGarry at his shoulder, "There is another way."

McGarry gestures for him to speak. Directing his question to Duff's nephew, Dennis says, "You have had military training, where?"

"Dublin."

"Doing?"

"The art and science of cannon."

Dennis says quietly to McGarry, "We need his knowledge."

"Hang him," Tiernan repeats staunchly, "or pike him, is what I say."

McGarry rubs his lips, then puts his hand up to thwart Boot's intention to grasp the young officer's forearm.

"Will you march with us, boy – teach our men on how to use the howitzers?"

Gifford, Dennis thinks, must feel like a fox after being asked to run with the hounds.

He stares at the ground as though an answer to his predicament is to be found there and then averts his hazel eyes skywards.

McGarry thinks the lad ought to waken up and snatch at the offer. As if somehow invigorated by McGarry's thoughts he says loudly, nervously and with false determination, "Yes. I'll do that, of course."

*

Crawfords' yard is strewn with detritus; broken wine bottles and glasses, wooden crates, broken chairs, torn curtains, sites of defecation, splashes of blood, the odour disgusting to Sally, so much so she brings her hand to her mouth, and gags on her way to the tiny flower garden Louise liked to maintain with her grandfather. It lay behind the stables, encircled by tall and unpruned yew trees, entered and exited by a red wicket gate, its colours flaked enough to show off its former lime green. Sally's return to the ruined home is her final one, the inside of the house she will not visit again, for it holds nothing apart from images of horror and terror – she has come to the garden to take something once promised to her by Louise, that she had either neglected to give her or had forgotten all about the promise.

The gate squeaks, claps into place after she passes through. The grass had been mown and its cuttings left to dry and discolour. Slates indicating animal graves are at the rear of the garden, under the young hazel tree, and is where she makes for – she feels it is wrong for her to be here. Now that the house is empty, she believes her open guest invitation has expired, withdrawn by old Mr Crawford who never hurt a fly; in light of what has happened, she cannot blame him. Mrs Crawford is a funny old fish – so mean she wouldn't permit you to cross her shadow for free. It's a good job that breathing is easy and free or our masters would be levying it. Mother doesn't like the Crawfords – jealous for them having such a privileged life and the Bible wounds further whenever the friar speaks of 'covetousness.'

There is shade under the hazel tree, coolish and comforting. The names on the graves are no more, and though Louise had told her many times, she remembers only Patch, the terrier with the gimpy hind leg. Close-by is a mound of quartz stones gotten for Louise by her grandfather, who liked to spin yarns. All of them are true, he would insist, for the most part. These crystal stones often covered ancient temples and tombs, and the druids referred to them as 'Frozen light.' Leprechauns use the stones as currency, he once said, but she noticed the smile he was hiding in the corner of his mouth and thought it a bubble burst.

She kneels and touches the cairn of pebbles, picking the smallest she could find, clasping it in her hand, praying the Lord's Prayer as she gripped it tightly…she does not know what the druids meant when they called quartz frozen light – she can only understand what she holds, a frozen teardrop for her to remember Louise.

*

Word arrives not long after the capture of the mail coach for the men to assemble for the march on Monasterevin. In the tavern Dennis notices McGarry squinting at the dispatch letter from a Captain Art O'Byrne of Nurney. He sees in his dim almost feral eyes the relief that this other man had assumed the leadership mantle. Dennis had met O'Byrne once and thought it enough. A man with blotched facial skin, a bland expression, the face of a banker, a spy, one face with many others behind it. But perhaps he is a good man, Dennis concedes, because he had judged people wrongly before, heeded unfounded gossip, and his own intuition occasionally failed him.

Hitherto Dennis understood McGarry to be a natural leader, rich in confidence, but now he realises that this only applies when he is at his forge, where he knows his craft, what needs doing. Forge and tavern his natural habitats and not always in that order.

The man's lips move but no words leave his mouth.

"Will you spake up and tell us what we're about," Boots says, pushing the burning candle across the table. McGarry begins quietly, "According to the orders, we've to prepare to move out – we're to take the main street – O'Byrne and his men will be taking the route into the town by the canal…another column is to advance on the turnpike…"

Something else, though. Dennis senses.

"Boots, go ready the men – will you do me a head count like a good man," McGarry says with a degree of languor.

They watch him leaving. Dennis realises that what is about to be said isn't for Tiernan's ears.

McGarry coughs and then begins to whisper, "Lord Dundas has offered an amnesty to the Kilcullen lads at Knockaulin Hill. For the surrender of their weapons they'll be allowed to return home safe and well to their families. Some are supposed to be dwelling upon the proposal. Things had gone well there at first in the fray but alas…"

"We're lost," Dennis says, recalling Elizabeth's warning.

'That eejit O'Byrne writes about court-martial and hanging traitors, those who flee our lines, and says we are to strongly remind our men of the cause.'

"Your thoughts?"

"He's a bleddy fool."

"And about our situation?"

"You mean how do we get out of this shite hole with our necks untouched?"

*

The boy

In the autumn of his childhood, before his blood began to simmer, he was apprenticed to Guiney the Blacksmith; long before the tide's white horses became as curved blades, and the incoming waves turned sand the colour of blood.

He was reddening iron at the forge, this boy of scarce years, when one day business fell into a chasm of near silence. Guiney's large hand rested as an anvil on his shoulder as he said. "Respect, lad. Does that priest of yours teach you nothing? Or is it because there's nothing between your ears to hold Godly words?"

There was extreme heat in the forge, the sizzling of water sprinkled over furnace coals created a dank and smoky odour. The pits of Hell, he'd imagined. Carty the wrought iron man had done the blessing, drawing a sharp look from Guiney and subsequently a high raising of Carty's broad shoulders, and an apologetic expression suggestive of his having momentarily forgotten himself. Guiney's forge needs no blessing from a catholic.

Roger rested his hammer on the anvil, the poker he was fashioning perhaps as close to perfect as he had thus far created. The drumbeat slow and low sounding trumpeted the cortege's approach. The smithies formed a line outside the forge. Across the way a bony tabby toyed with a field mouse under a cottage window. A pair of magpies rested on a low wall, then raucously cawed in protest at being disturbed and flew to the nearest tree. Distant cloud imaged that of a man with a long nose and a broad forehead, a woolly black periwig streaked grey.

The lowering of heads, of calloused hands making the sign of the cross, as the cortege passed by.

4 dapple grey horses, plumed large with breeze quivering blue, flagged at bladder filled skies, towed a white carriage dressed in gilded trims and lantern towers in each corner.

Sturdy iron braces on the wheels, made in forge, clattered over pebbles, chorused the clip-clopping.

Trailed by slow walking followers fancily geared up, stepping over dung droppings of market bound cattle.

Young Roger McGarry could tell the skies wanted to pour,

but they held back their tears – or piss – for the man in the floral adorned coffin was deserving if that were to drop.

Not that he knew the man. God, no. But he knew them, their kind. The reason most of the shops and the tavern in town were closed, a person of importance was signalling his status to Saint Peter and wanted the push of the people at his back…*so much for every soul being equal.*

The forge remained open, for the late magistrate's Irish yeomanry wanted a batch of horseshoes. And Guiney being in their unit would fail many others before even considering to disappoint the Ancient Hibernians. Luke Carty his foreman, the man who'd fashioned magnificent gates for the gentry, recently a father to a son Ted, when Guiney was away and sometimes he was away often, battered choice pike heads into being – all they needed was Roger's father to add the ash pikestaff, for a weapon to be poised ready. For the hands of death to wield.

The tabby began its blood play and tore at the mouse till it had severed its head, poking both parts to ensure it was not one of those mice which had eluded him previously.

They waited until the beat and fall of hooves was out of earshot, before returning to the clanging of hammer. Later as he filled pails of water he imagined the magistrate lying in the coffin, his long life, the people he had sent to the gallows, and thought how the Bible said everyone should be treated equally, and he considered how a wise man like a magistrate could know those words and yet did not think this also applied to his good self. Like drifting leaves Roger's thoughts then pondered on the mourners; they would talk, perhaps laughing at each other's regaling of the magistrate's life stories, deeds and misdeeds, assuming solemnity as the horses turned at the pillars to enter the burial ground.

Then the paid keeners would sound and paid for tears would

muddy the truth, that someone had died whose presence Christ would welcome. A decent man, a kindly soul, fair minded – the grieving would be mighty, yet not long afterward, the inns' floorboards would bounce gladly with dancing, singing, smoking, drinking, and while this was going on, Carty and Sixsmith would hide their pike heads in a field beyond a canal bridge; ash was scarce.

Never returned to, the pikes remained buried, doused in fish oil, because months later Roger's father perished after slipping under a cartwheel while assisting to free it from feculent bog. While Carty a year after McGarry's death had drowned in the River Barrow, after weeds had wrapped themselves around his ankles. It was said. But Roger suspected that Carty was murdered, the perpetrators his mother and two of his older sisters; his body had gash wounds, and the doctor said these were cuts effected by those retrieving the body from the river weeds. But it was not the first-time women of their small home had slashed out at a man who'd caused them dreadful shame and suffering.

*

Darkness. Dennis stands outside the tavern and inhales and exhales the breath of camp smoke, listens to the low talk, bursts of loud laughter, the stirring of their few horses, feeling tipsy. He crosses the road and goes a short depth into the woods to relieve himself. They are about five miles from Monasterevin and would soon commence the march, to begin the assault at 4 a.m. The strength of their column Tiernan estimates at 550. Others from Nurney and Kildangan would perhaps reach roughly the same tally. About 1,300 souls would be in battle within a few hours.

Intelligence reported that Captain Winter had withdrawn his small force of Suffolk Fencibles and 9th Dragoons from

Monasterevin, leaving a mere 80 yeoman infantry and cavalry to defend the town.

Weight of numbers might be enough to see the job through, he hopes, buttoning his fly.

What then?

Only God knows.

A balmy night. His clothes sticky. A light breeze, the caress of a wandering soul, touches his forehead. Dennis hates the pitch black of night. How it presses in about a body with its essence, makes him blind. Lanterns, rush-light, candlelight, turf-fires…he is away from these now, for minutes, looking at them pushing against the blackness, hearing the voices, the snoring, the stirring of horses, a dog whelping after being struck. Creaks of dawn are a show of splintered light. *What if I simply mounted up and rode home to Elizabeth and forgot about this trouble. Jay, she's right. There's no good will come out of this. It's the tally of total disarray.*

*

The column's infantry marches in ranks of three, cavalry to the front. Roger and Boots front 23 cavalrymen, flintlocks wedged in leather belts or waist ropes, swords sheathed. Dennis rides up and down the flanks, eases his horse alongside the marching men: men bearing pikes across their shoulders, some with flintlocks shoved into their britches, others carrying muskets used for shooting fowl, more with swords in scabbards that dance against their hips, those towards the rear carry pitchforks and scythes – last of all, farther back, the baggage wagons ferrying their meagre supplies. While at battle, the butchers will slaughter cows rustled from landlords' fields. A realisation bites at his marrow that not all of the men, including his good self, will be alive to dine this evening. Consoles himself by muttering a phrase, 'What's meant for you will not pass you by.' In other words, your fate is yours alone to contend with, to accept. Not to be ready for it, for there's never a readiness where death is concerned, for when its hammer eventually falls, tis still a mighty blow.

He acknowledges those who call out, fixing a smile for them. A travelling caravan of bright greenery. On its way to butcher and be butchered on this 25th day of May. A Friday he will long remember, he suspects. Dust rises around their feet. A drum occasionally taps to help the men keep in the right step. About as much soldiering as any of them had previously experienced. Flags in the stifling heat cling limply to their poles – the green patterned with the golden harp, the Fitgerald with its red cross on white…appear to shy away from the day.

'Crom abu,' he whispers, 'Crom abu,' he mutters, a war cry of Kildare men from the 15th century. He knew his history, perhaps it would have spared him better not to know a whit of it. Or perhaps only a smidgen so as not to make him care.

*

The Ironmonger's son

During an evening as linnets breeze across a purple skyline, Roger asks, waving away puffs of pipe smoke, "Can you read atall?"

"Not atall…ah, no, Sir, but I can make out some letters."

"So you're an x man."

"Like my father, my mother, x marks my spot."

"You should learn to read."

"I tried to with the hedge teacher, but he said I was word blind, that I wrote my letters arsewards and talked nothing only pure manure. Which is why I try not to talk too much."

Roger chuckles, studies his pipe's chimney, "Ye didn't get along so."

"You can read, can't you?"

"Why ask a question that you already know the answer to?"

"Habit…I don't trust my ears, not all of the time at any rate, Sir. There are fellas who'd have no trouble atall in convincing you that carrots are green and spuds are turnips."

Roger slices a sliver of beef and another, "Your father was the same…"

Reflects silently. *Tell him something and he'd question you umpteen times before the day was done – if it were true what you had told him earlier: was it you who told me that, who's this that did that, is it true, really, can you read…checking if I was certain of my colours…*

"I believe Sir that reading is like talking, both can land you in a pile of horseshit."

"For sure…but the war of the words, lad…we're dealing with aristocrats, a bloody hereditary power in that fecking monarchy… and we need to speak their language…because they're not wanting to learn ours. If you could read, you would have surely read of Thomas Paine and his book The Rights of Man – tis in print 8 years, now, I think."

"I've heard of him and some of his writings, and he's right – this is why we rebelled, so we poor folk could be better off."

"You heard. Y'see…it's a bit like the Bible; you hear the words falling from a priest's mouth and those of other shysters, but if you read it yourself, wouldn't that be a good thing for you. To take the matter into your own hands. Of deciding for yourself what you believe in, or do not, eh?"

"Like I said. Errah too much reading is like too much talking; there's too much room for lying."

"There's no sense in talking sense to you, lad. You're your father to the core, full of mutinous bones."

Silence.

"Sir, you now and then speak very ill of the clergy. But not every egg in the basket is cracked."

McGarry farts and says, "Young Carty; you talk too much."

*

The town yields easily enough, quicker than expected, with few casualties – one dead, several wounded to four yeomanry piked to death within mere minutes of battle. Yet, Dennis worries that the capture had been too easily a done deal. He knows Winter, a man too belligerent to consider taking a step back, unless there's someone who truly bent his ear.

Monasterevin is a larger town than either Clane or Prosperous and a stronger resistance was anticipated, even from a depleted force – he can't quite suss the reason for his uneasiness. To him, the feeling seems like some awkwardness he might have with Elizabeth: he would know something is bothering her but could never accurately guess the source. In the end he has to be told by her, which invariably worsens the situation.

You shouldn't have to be told.

There's nothing worse than knowing there's a problem and not knowing what it is, he thinks. Agitation brings on nauseousness, of drink turned sour in his belly. Even his steed is spooked. His eyes wide and wild. Dennis dismounts, ties the reins of his charge to a hook in a wall and helps to carry a wounded pike man to a cart.

Smoke from houses set alight breezes away from the better direction, not veiling them with fog, as hoped; a breeze can turn.

Of a sudden, just as the sun's midday glares their eyes, an

enfilade from yeomen lurking in the upstairs of a draper's shop, tears through the air. In the volley, men drop, their spattered blood and shattered bone lie on the dust, unblinking eyes in sundered bodies. Images imprinted in Dennis's mind within an instant. A gale blows within him, and an inner voice tells him to act.

It is a signal, too.

For the rising thunder of hooves, the yells, the glint on the edge of the sabres, as bright as silver on shop display; a second volley of shots from the drapery is loud and ugly; clouds of cordite drape the window frames.

Dennis hurries to his horse, mounts, and faces into the charging enemy, his sword poised, ready to lead an attack. His horse rears, half-turns, affording Dennis the sight of a retreating force, chased by lead, sword, and lance. Beside him, a man ships a ball to his right eye, another in the throat – these are deadly caresses.

Surveying the fencibles with intense hatred as they cut a swathe through the fleeing ranks, he nudges his horse about and digs his heels hard against its flanks. Triggers his flintlock into the face of an approaching enemy. A man he knows, who owns good land, a bigot, an Orangeman. O'Rourke falls from his saddle and is dragged along the ground before losing his foot from the stirrups. A shot whizzes past Dennis's ear.

Then, he turns, having caught the contagiousness of panic. He feels neither shame nor guilt, just a wild desire to put a distance between himself and the battle.

*

Roots

"Tell me what else you know of this man Paine."

A cough escapes Roger, a catch in his throat, another cough. His eyes water. He stands, palm of his hand flat on his chest, sighs.

Carty hands him a tankard of water and Roger slurps from it and draws the back of his hand across his lips. Sighs…Nature is slowly throttling me to death, he thinks.

He breathes deeply, exhales, sips his water. His eyes turn to the sky, at the lone eagle beginning its swoop to earth, to satisfy its hunger. Picks up his pipe and pockets it.

Brings his toe to his brackish bedding of hay and mutters drily that even an oul donkey has its bed changed more often than himself. Bleakly, he says, "Death, boy is a work in train…"

Creaking knee joints as he lowers himself to his bedding, fussing with the hay, fluffing it as though it were a pillow.

"Paine," he says, sounding jaded, "wanted to ban the right of succession of the first born – he wanted to get rid of aristocratic titles – and for the like of us like meself he wanted to look after our ageing, giving 6 pounds to those aged between fifty to sixty and ten pounds to those older than that…per annum…wouldn't it be handsome indeed?"

"For doing what kind of work?"

"Getting old and being old."

"Money for doing nothing, is that it?"

"Do you think getting on in years is easy…it's far from it…you've heard my bones creaking and cracking, seen my fecking knee give way, how I get out of breath, and break out in the sweats…ageing is God's crime against humanity."

Carty goes to speak but thinks wiser of it. Roger says Paine was sentenced for seditious libel against the majesties and sentenced to swing for it…but he was in France and had the good sense to remain there.

"What does sedit…mean?"

"Causing people to rebel against the monarchy, like we did."

"We're fecked so," says more to himself than Roger.

"Paine brought Paine to everyone."

Roger hesitates, expecting Carty to smile at his pun of sorts, but instead the young man frowns, his thoughts evidently elsewhere, riding the waves of the lines on his forehead.

He says, "I better set to cleaning my Bess, the barrel is filthy, and-"

"Powder?"

"Enough."

Carty's blunderbuss had stood out from the very many others in their formations, in that it wasn't rusty and its barrel spotless; he took pride in his father's firelock.

"Rabbit, rabbit, that's for dinner, and a few spuds, how does that sound, young Carty?

"Fine, Sir."

"Drop the Sir, would you, for the love of the Lord."

"Will you drop young and Carty and call me Edward."

"It's Ted, isn't it, a buachaill."

"Give us a whistle when it's ready."

*

Later, back at the tavern, he learns of the 63 killed in action, a mere 2 were dragoons, in addition to 8 horses. And of McGarry there is no sign. Dennis wonders if he has survived. Tiernan? The men now at their base camp amount to no more than a couple of hundred, the majority having retired to Kildare town to relate a sad tale to its citizens.

Apart from the loss of life, over 200 pikes, 8 guns, 2 large blunderbusses and a variety of old guns and swords were lost. A quick tally is all, the proper findings won't ever have a true count.

Pikes dropped because it is awkward to take flight with them, as opposed to carrying swords and guns. You can't blame a man for wanting to hasten from turmoil, from impending death.

Unable to sit with his thoughts he ventures outside – searching for quiet acres of the heart, the act of following his feet will at least distract him somewhat.

Bloodstained banners lie draped across the branches of hawthorn, setting white against red. An unlucky tree, cursed by the fairies, the wee men. Legends of old. The mood of the men is dark and sullen and they wear the dejected faces of losers in battle. There is not even the mildest scent of a better day ahead. A smell of tobacco smoke from clay pipes reaches his nostrils, watering his eyes.

A woman is sowing an attempted suicide cut on a young man's forearm. A man with steel wool hair holds a cloth to his eye socket. Another has lost an arm and stares at the empty space; his features etched in pain.

Raised voices cut through the flat and tainted atmosphere.

'Catch him!'

Dennis hurries around the corner of the cattle byre and sees the young officer Gifford lying on the ground.

"The bastard was running away; I put an end to his galloping,' a sentry accuses.

Gifford bleeds profusely from the corner of his mouth. Abrasions mark his high cheekbones. Before Dennis can utter a word, pikes are driven with brute force into the lad's chest and midriff. Curses rise high above Gifford's screams. Horrified, Dennis stares at the pikes hoisting the victim into the air, as though toasting him to the heavens, balancing Gifford's writhing so as not to let him fall to the ground. Raucous laughter and screams of malicious delight from the onlookers.

Oh, sweet Jesus.

*

Two days after the battle for Monasterevin, as the early morning mist clears, his force arrives at the outskirts of the town. Duff dispatches an advance party and views their progress through his telescope, aware of the rumblings within his company, fatigued and hungry, bickering with each other over nothings. Beckons the paymaster to his side, still gazing through lens, and says, "Pay the men…double…"

"Double pay, Sir."

"All ranks."

"Only, Sir…there isn't enough in our treasury…"

"Without paying the officers…is there?"

"I would imagine so."

"Don't imagine. Exclude myself also from your reckonings," he says, lowering the 'scope.

The paymaster nods.

Privates earn a shilling a day, a Colonel 32 of these – Duff thinks to make it up to his officers, but refrains from mentioning this, for he promises nothing unless he is certain he can follow his word to the letter. Right now he needs no rancour coursing through the veins of his company. As it is, the daily roll call revealed that 7 men had deserted. If he doesn't stop the haemorrhaging it could place matters in a precarious position. One can count on loyalty to the Crown, but only for so long. It's important to have his officers impress upon their charges that they are fighting for the lives of their families, for law and order, for peace – if this is not achieved then everything else will collapse into chaos. Yield as much as misery as had the *sans culottes*, those damned French anarchists.

He is content that the journey has been briskly achieved. There was not much evidence of rebellion along the route. Indeed, he is more than surprised to have travelled the distance without meeting even token confrontation. His counterparts in the various towns along the march had informed him of skirmishes with the Popish rebels, but none of these had taken long to quell. Indeed there were towns and village unaffected by rebellion.

The county of Kildare is different, it appears. Wexford, also. Rumours sail up and down the country – but nothing, Duff understands, is certain in war. The fact that he thinks of the uprising as a war draws him up short. He corrects himself: it is not a war – these are acts of high treason.

His thoughts are that the rebellion is an epidemic of sporadic outbreaks of mob violence – contagious and nowhere near being of an organised and cohesive nature. Then, Duff surmises, the rebel leaders had been arrested in the days preceding the insurgency. A blessing, for if the traitors had had their leaders, perhaps…

His scouts return to say, accompanied by a troop of Suffolk Fencibles, that Monasterevin is secure. He tells his men they can rest for the night there and fill their tankards. His spirits buoyed by the prospect of a decent meal and the knowledge that the rebels' advance was curtailed without causing deficiencies in his resources.

Too fatigued to join his officer colleagues for drinks, after the debriefing and plan for the morrow, in one of the big houses owned by the gentry, Duff retires to his quarters and drafts a brief report at his desk for the morning barge to Dublin. The main route to the city is too volatile and uncertain to entrust a dispatch rider to make it there safely.

To confirm to his Lordships his good haste, his seven pieces of cannon, the augmentation to his force, totalling 700 men – of the fact he marches on Kildare in the morn confident of success, where he hopes to meet with his nephew, a fine fellow…Who had been due to engage with him close to Abbeyliex.

*

Sally had been angry with Louise for a whole day; she couldn't remember being angry with anyone for so long in her whole life. All because of that spell in the cathedral grounds and Louise's hiding in the creepiest and darkest corner of the saint's kitchen – how could she do that to her? Didn't she know there were huge spiders, perhaps rats lurking in those corners?

Ghosts, even? She hadn't answered to her name and when she decided to, she snuck out of the kitchen, grabbed Sally's elbow and shouted, 'Boo!'

Sally wet herself a little and her heart jumped up her throat so she couldn't speak beyond the scream her soul had thrown out. After her anger cooled, she made her way up town intending to visit her friend. She could be at home, too afraid of all that is going on to venture out. Her nana is strict, too. Her wicked oul puss would put a banshee to flight.

There was commotion and burning houses and a man was hanging from a gibbet in the square. She was curious to see him up close because Jack had told her what he had witnessed: the man had begged for mercy, how the priest had stood by and prayed for God to forgive his sins but did nothing to try and stop the killing. Like God he had given the people free choice.

She had not gone too close, for birds' pecked at the dead man and he had begun to smell. The entire scene horrible and yet fascinating and full of intrigue – the dead man was alive yesterday and dead today, but the dead self just looked empty. A husk of acorn…she failed to make sense of how it could be so; take her cat too, Mousie, when she died, she felt she was looking at an empty vessel of sorts. Definitely wasn't her Mousie. There was really nothing to be sad over, was there…she would ask Louise to share her thoughts. Most people usually cry when someone dies but she hadn't when Mousie died, nor when Granny had gone to meet her maker. She'd tried to squeeze the tears then, but her eyes were as dry as the plains; she could only pretend to look sad and forlorn. It felt like a sin but so too would a smile.

Sally dallied via the square to reach Louise's house - there is another route through a laneway, but this is not a nice way: strange men lurk about and even before this trouble began, it could be dangerous.

Sally Downey preferred the sun when it wasn't this hot. But she loved the fact that rain wasn't keeping her indoors. Her forehead and arms were sunburned and last night she'd found the burning made it too uncomfortable for her to sleep. She'd wondered if Louise had got too much sun or if she'd found a spider in her long, lovely hair? This morning, she had made up her mind to speak with her. She will remain her friend if she promises never again to scare the wits out of her, and not to ever go hiding in dark places. And to answer her name whenever it's called.

No one paid her any heed. She'd never seen the town so packed with people: sitting to and leaning against walls and in the shade of the market's trees. Women tended to the huge and steaming cooking pots. She smelt the stew and it whetted her appetite. Men drilled on the road, simultaneously thrusting the air with their pikes. An instructor called for one to hold tight onto the shaft till he could see the white of his knuckles, till he thought the bone would show through the skin. Ash: she smelt the remains of a dead fire, the smoke of living ones, of ale and whiskey and tobacco from clay pipes and everywhere too, the smell of sweat and animal.

"Where are you off ta?" A woman said to her.

At first, Sally failed to recognise her and then she said, "Hannah…"

Sally thought, "What is she doing here? And how come she's

wearing that lovely blue bonnet?" Sally had admired it on Mrs Crawford – its colour lessened the strain in her face and felled some years away from her hard features. Louise loved that bonnet, loved her grandparents, especially her grandfather. Everyone liked him but Mrs Crawford had a reputation for being short with people. Father said she was an egg short of the full dozen. Louise was holidaying with her grandparents – her third summer to spend in Kildare, their second as best friends.

"To see Louise," Sally said.

Hannah stood unsteadily. Her beautiful green eyes with the flecks of brown were misted. She wore lipstick and those earrings…

Oh, Lord. They belong to Mrs Crawford too

"Go back to your oul fella – tell the bucko that Hannah McGarry was asking for him," she said, winking at the woman beside her.

Whatever does she mean?

"Move along now before I give you a root up your bony behind."

Sally hurried on, using the people milling around to hide herself from Hannah, proceeding with a sense of growing dread.

Looking up the lane where Louise lived, Sally slowed and next took tentative steps forward. Every step brought the broken windows and the gaping doorway into sharper focus. Not a sinner here. Nothing except a few crows perching on top of the keep. And a silence that chilled to her very marrow.

Broken trellis's and trodden red roses garlanded the entrance. She caught their sweet fragrance as she stepped over them into the hallway. The silence of the bees loud in her ears.

"Louise?" she called.

Silence.

"It's me, Sally."

Silence.

"Louise!"

Something then. A noise. She couldn't be certain what caused it. Upstairs, perhaps of furniture being moved?

"Mister Crawford...Mrs Crawford," she said, a shakiness to her voice.

She intended to call again, passing the open doors to rooms either side of her, not pausing to take in their destruction, when she reached the bottom of the staircase. The amount of the blood on the stairs, the cracked banisters, its absent spindles, the splintered ones, kept her voice in check.

"Louise...it's me, Sally!" she said aloud, now frightened

Again, that noise. Louder, this time.

Sally breathed in deeply. She'd felt a thousand cold fingers run along her spine. On the small first landing, stood Mrs Crawford. Her eyes wide, hands open and held by her side. Tears falling. Her face puce coloured.

"Sally," she murmured, almost in a croak, holding up her blood-stained hands.

Sally backed away.

"Don't...' Mrs Crawford said, "Sally. Help..."

The mention of her name, as though it were dipped in the woman's most terrible anguish, prompted Sally into full flight.

She is at home now, present at table, showing her mother the small quartz teardrop she had taken as a memento of her stricken friend, from the garden, at rest on her palm. After the lump in her throat passes, Elizabeth quietly and solemnly admires it. From outside there is a sonorous gust of wind that comes and goes, and into the silence, Sally says, "Is that what Louise's grandfather would call a portent."

"Bring the pots to the cesspit, good girl...and don't lose your teardrop."

*

Hannah

There he is now with the snooty Lord Muck head on him, stuck up nose and she his good wife walking beside him, a scut, small breasted craythur – what does a fine man like him see in her?

Nothing much for his hands to grab or his mouth to play on – bad cess to her. He wouldn't want to now, so he wouldn't, walk by me without bidding me a hello, and a biteen of a smile to show he appreciates the secret we do share between us.

I don't believe it. He's going to walk on without so much as a glance. I'll fix that boyo.

"Dennis," Hannah beckons.

He remains steadfast in ignoring her after she calls him again. Elizabeth stiffens, eases his hand from her elbow, and says, "That amadan of a hoor wants you – I'll walk on ahead of you to Crawfords. You should ignore her as you would a pile of cow dung in our path."

"Is she? I didn't hear."

He glances over at Hannah, who smiles.

Elizabeth snaps, "How do you know her?"

"She's Roger's sister – she works for the Crawfords. They only recently hired her – against my wishes, I might add."

"Why? How is you know her well enough to return her address. Fond address it appears? And you think me stupid to believe the Crawfords would confide in you about who they should hire?"

Elizabeth's eyes bore into his and then back off. She will not grill him here, in this mess of a place, where people have lost the run of themselves, close to where a dead man hangs and sways from a lime tree.

"Roger told me, Elizabeth; she comes across as a wicked and vile soul if what he says is even fractionally correct."

"An expensive bonnet – they must be paying her very well. Better than I was for doing a maid's work for the Cannington gentry."

"I doubt it."

"I was being sarcastic – doesn't she keep fine company indeed? Mind yourself there, Dennis, you could end up between that pair of fat thighs and never be heard tell of again."

"For God's sake, Elizabeth. She probably knows something about Roger."

"Perhaps,' she responds, "but what does it matter?"

"I should indeed go over. She might have news of what happened in the Crawford household, too. The whys of it."

"Shall I accompany you, would you like that?" she says, though she has no intention of presenting herself to such sluttish company.

"No, God, no… she will not tell me anything in front of you."

"You do indeed know her so well. Next you'll be telling me she can read and write."

"Not nearly as well as you," his words cold.

Ah, she thinks, taking in the tiniest shade of crimson in his cheeks, the dart of his eyes to the ale puddle close to his feet. Hmm. *He wouldn't dare – or has he already dared to?*

*

He watches his wife step this way and that to avoid brushing against people, intent on getting to the Crawfords to see what had scared the wits out of poor Sally.

That bitch, Hannah. Out to make trouble.

She has a good sup in her. Though younger than Elizabeth by a decade, she looks older. The head of someone who has slept off a feed of ale and wakened to start afresh a new feast. Red haired, heavily freckled, eyes cut like stone, a fleshy beautiful lump of a woman. She is missing a front tooth, and he supposes it's the result of a drunken brawl.

He stares at her companion until she understands to bring her ears to a distance.

"Are you trying to cause trouble for me with Elizabeth?" he says, gripping Hannah's upper arm.

"Let go of me."

"You're lucky it's not your neck I grabbed. Have you news of Roger?" he says, noticing black brogues on her feet – she who had never owned fine shoes prior to the uprising.

"No. I would say, kind Sir, that he is running around trying to think of a way to save his neck and leaving the fighting to the real men."

"The Crawfords?"

"Oh, I heard some of the lads went in and broke up the furniture – that's all I know."

"The bonnet you're wearing, those shoes?"

"Mrs Crawford gave it me," she replies, touching its frilled rim, "such a kind woman she is."

"Shouldn't you be there now, helping them to put their home right?"

"With all the shenanigans going on. Hardly. I wouldn't miss this excitement, Dennis. Sure, when will it come again?"

"Do you think they'll want your services when this is all over?"

Hannah sighs, "We can go down the laneway – I think you need a bit of cheer."

In daylight? Fleeting images of their previous liaisons fired his blood. What if Elizabeth returns? He could say Hannah had brought him to see her wounded brother. For sure, she would know it was a lie, but it wouldn't be a living one unless in a fit of remorse he cries out his sin. She is worth the carrying of guilt.

He could not reason against his lust.

*

The grief-stricken woman embraces Elizabeth as though she is close family and not as a stranger whom she knows only to see; they have never given each other the grace of a 'Good morning.'

George Crawford lies on his bed in the couple's bedroom. Elizabeth thinks the green lighted candles on a dresser are somehow incongruous; one burns brightly, the other guttering and dying off in a cloud of smoke, touching as a halation the bright candle, effecting the wick to sway as a bog reed. Upon drawing close to the sight of the dead man, Elizabeth makes the sign of the Cross. Such a tortuous countenance on the poor man's face, she thinks. The widow did what she could to make him presentable, but he is not fit for his wake.

"He was a good man," Nellie says, "one of the better ones. He didn't deserve this ending. Not him, my poor George."

"No, he didn't deserve this fate," agrees Elizabeth, modulating her tone to kindness.

Elizabeth asks of Louise.

"Oh, she is sleeping."

"Sleeping?"

Where the hell has Dennis gotten to?

Hardly to see McGarry.

"How did you – the rebels?" Elizabeth asks as they exit the room to visit Louise.

"I hid. Shame on me, under the privet hedge, crawled in as far as it was possible and they came out and looked around and not seeing me went on and took the horses while others ransacked the house and robbed us – even our maid, Hannah. I know the faces I saw and the names of a few – as God is my judge…"

Elizabeth finds no words when her eyes fall upon the child, for she knows death's touch. She has a fever, the blood drained from her face, her beautiful hair matted with perspiration, her breathing shallow and rasping.

"I'm too afraid to go and look for a doctor," Nellie says very quietly, "they'd murder me, wouldn't they, Elizabeth? And I would not know where to look for one, do you?"

"Doctor Phillips, perhaps – Nellie – though he could be off somewhere."

The likelihood is that he is gone with the rebels. And not of his own accord.

Elizabeth leans over Louise. The child's eyes are shut. She notices the scratch marks on her chin, the blood stains on the sheet.

"I couldn't do a thing to save her, you see – she had left me to go and get her doll – you believe me, Elizabeth, don't you? I heard her scream and I knew; I knew…next they were out looking for me – get the oul one they said. They didn't search too hard because they were afraid of missing out on the spoils in the house."

"I need to find my husband, Nellie; we have to get a doctor. We must."

"Yes."

"I won't be long, I promise."

What the bleddy hell is keeping that lad?

"Elizabeth?"

"Yes?"

"Whatever am I going to say to Patrick and Ann Marie?"

The child's parents, Elizabeth assumes.

"Dampen her forehead,' she says over the swell of emotion in her throat, 'I must hurry."

*

Reinforcements. A message had been received to expect a short delay because of their hanging of two rebel stragglers found half-drunk in a ditch. Duff sits on a canvas chair by the canal, watching the troops prepare for disembarkation. In the broiling sunshine some of the horses have gotten in a right lather, even before the midday sun lights on their backs. After the fresh horses arrive, he intends to issue an order for the most exhausted of the charges to be given another day's respite. Some of the men are worse for wear, too. But these he cannot spare. Each finger on a musket's trigger, each hand on a sword's hilt, each trained man is needed.

Clouds of midges above the canal waters, ripples to indicate the presence of fish.

Trout, he supposes. He stands and goes to the bank, throws in a stone. His right knee causes him a random flash of pain which always worsens after he sits for too long.

He holds his hands out and studies his knuckles. Incipient pain there whenever he makes a fist or grips hard on an object. Old age, approaching storms.

Brings to his mind that saying of his father's, 'Old bones tell no lies, they're the devil in disguise.'

Incapacity is a while away yet – he would have time to do his duty and punish those who dared to attack his Majesty's forces, to wrest away land and properties not theirs, to kill.

Vaguely, he hears his name, it jolts him into turning about. Facing Captain Samuel Cannington, he returns the other's salute.

"Sir, I have received grievous news."

"Speak up, man – has there been a reversal? The reinforcements-"

"Are almost present, Sir – they're reached the turnpike. I came on ahead."

'What's troubling you?'

A leave request at this hour? He does not look the sort to let anything flinch him from his hour of call.

"It concerns your nephew, Sir."

"Michael?"

He feels a wash of something cold slip over his heart, like an incoming tide.

"I regret to say that we have found his body, Sir."

His blood froze around his heart, a pain pierced, nausea pushed bile to his mouth. "Good God!"

"I-"

"Bring me, now."

"Horse!" the officer calls, clicking his fingers.

Minutes later, he dismounts in front of the medical tent and enters. A surgeon wearing a blood-spattered apron brings him to a covered trestle table. Flies, stench of sweet blood, elsewhere a deep soulful crying from a man undergoing the saw running its serrated teeth above his kneecap.

'Leave me be,' Duff says to the surgeon and Cannington.

He blesses himself and lifts a corner of the grey blanket. Merciful heavens! This creature bears but a slight resemblance to his nephew, but it is indeed poor Michael. His face is bloated; blood caked in and around his wounds. Birds have gone with his eyes.

He feels his legs give and leans his thighs against the rim of the table for support.

Michael, who used to visit him every summer, who wanted to become a leather merchant like his uncle, who was the son he never had. His brother's son. Christ! *The news will break Charles.*

*

The farce at Monasterevin ultimately convinces Roger there is no hope of success for the rebellion. Debacle persuasion. Courage by itself will never win a war. He finds it hard to believe he was once so thoroughly convinced the rebellion would succeed. An abundance of lies and rumour fed the army such false hope. A simple thought-out ploy by a military man had outdone them and put to flight a force many times larger, if poorly equipped and inadequately trained.

We're rabble, Roger McGarry whispers to himself as he rides behind Tiernan and their leader, O'Byrne, to Knockaulin Hill outside old Kilcullen where Lord Dundas has offered pardon for those who surrender their arms. Generous terms in light of the death and destruction woven by their side in the rebellion. *Decent terms by the victor.*

An oath of allegiance to the Crown would have to be uttered on bended knee if not heart, and a solemn promise never again to lift a finger against crown forces.

They'd set out for the hill on the strength of a rumour, a prayer and whiskey before dawn, sticking to the night so as to evade capture by the cavalry patrols with whom there is little prospect of pardon unless one carries a protection letter. Even so it is not beyond neither cavalry nor yeoman officer to ignore official documentation and concoct a fresh offence which they would later declare to have nullified the order.

They are done, defeated again, the years of striving to banish the English will run into the approaching century and beyond.

Lord Edward Fitzgerald, their leader, their military strategist, veteran of war in the Americas had died in prison from his wounds, gained from resisting his capture in Dublin. Roger had learned of this from O'Brien an hour ago, a rumour had grown into a fact, and yes – *we are done.* Sixpence saw it coming…*thank God I heeded his advice some part and prepared for where I now find myself.*

McGarry joins the rebels already lined up in orderly queues to bend the knee and surrender their arms. Not all of his weapons are on his person, he has a flintlock, a blunderbuss, a sword - prior to setting out he had wrapped in hessian and hidden three muskets, a flintlock, ammunition, gunpowder, daggers and a dozen pike heads in furze, under the eyes of Carty and Talbot. Rainy day arms, Carty had said. And he was right, McGarry acknowledged, there might come a day. A man will need a hideaway, a lair, a place where he can keep out of sight to allow time for people to forget him. Time is God's eraser.

The mood of the men descending the hill is lighter than those ascending. The absence of arms, the sheaf of protection, appears to have shed a load of worry from their faces, a weight that had humped their shoulders. They are like men who fully understand their good fortune to walk away from the noose and from having their heads pitch capped, their backs flogged, a sabre pushed. A menu of punishments from which the bastards choose, if shooting is considered too a quick a death.

"Name," the officer says, as Roger approaches the long trestle table outside the tent.

Brass paper weights prevent the breeze from stealing the records.

"Roger McGarry, from Clane," he says, volunteering the information as he had overheard the questions being asked of the man before him.

He espies O'Byrne and Tiernan making their way down the hill.

"From the Kildare rebels?" the officer says, pointing at a name on a ledger under his sergeant's eyes.

Before Roger can reply, the officer says., "According to Captains O'Byrne and Tiernan, you're of the same rank as they and one other by the name of Dennis Downey and are leaders of the Kildare town insurgents. Others from there have handed in their weapons.

They assure me that the laying down of arms will occur as soon as possible on the plains. Is it true?"

"So, they promoted me here at this very table, in front of your good selves," Roger tries lightly, "that was most uncommonly generous of them."

"Lord Dundas has given instructions for the leaders of the Kildare rebels to organise a handover for weapons to General Duff – he has despatched a letter to the General to this effect."

"Who is General Duff?" McGarry says, remembering then, a remembering that chilled his very marrow.

"Do you wish to hand over your weapons now?"

"Will I receive a protection notice?"

"Your so-called Captain O'Byrne has a temporary order for himself and those in his company."

"He is gone on ahead of me."

The officer says, with a weary look down the queue, waving the next man forward, "Those are the sort of men you chose to run with. Are they not?"

"I-".

"You should give over your arms and hurry on after him."

The three unarmed men ride somewhat uneasily in each other's company. Tiernan like McGarry is upset with Art O'Byrne for giving their names and titles to the officer but has not put him to task. After all, he is the one carrying the protection order and rides a stout black horse that could leave theirs far behind. O'Byrne engages the men in conversation, concerning their plans – it is best to have their men hand over their weapons in their camp at Gibbet Rath…we can-

"Some might not want to surrender the cause," Tiernan casually remarks.

McGarry remains silent. There is, he observes, the illusion of a cross carved dark into a drystone wall, as he approaches the illusion shows it genuine self – they are merely crevices, a break between stones. No less. No more than.

Tiernan mouths again about the doubters at the rath, to which Roger dismisses harshly

"Those who remain at the rath don't want the war to continue – the others less inclined for the bloodletting to stop, won't stay. By being at Knocknaulin, we have said our words worth. Yes."

Tiernan grunted.

"Well man, shut it."

Reaching Sunnyhill the Curragh Plains spreads out in an apron of grassland and gorse, lone rowan trees. Along a hoof pocked trail penned in by furze, Tiernan who is leading the way, raises himself in his saddle and looking back at O'Byrne says, "You could have kept your mouth shut about us, Art."

"Why? Didn't I own up myself and say I was a captain?"

McGarry says, "More fool you, then."

Tiernan says, "Slip a noose about your own neck, boy, but not mine."

"He knew who I was – didn't the other men there say it to him to get in his good books."

McGarry says lowly, "I don't like the scent of this at all."

Silence.

McGarry considers mentioning Duff and his late nephew but decides it's a bit of news best kept to himself for the time being. He says, "What fecking hope had we, Art… with you in charge?"

Tiernan erupts in laughter. O'Byrne too, albeit nervously. McGarry joins in. Three laughing men under the sun, among the gold kissed furze and the bleached and bleating sheep, parched souls in their own right.

*

He is home, seated at the table, fingertips to his temple, eyes turned to the window, the garden, his father bringing a bucket of water to his horse in the stable. A rhubarb tart cools on the ledge, covered by a cloth to ward against flies and midges.

Elizabeth is moments in from the outhouse, still feeling sickly and suffering from diarrhoea after seeing to Mister Crawford's funeral. No one would sell her a coffin. Sack cloth made do. Gravediggers took turns to hew the hard earth, to shovel a hillock into being beside the grim opening. Garlic and bluebells fragranced the air, magpies were raucous, the sun beat down, the blackness of a sour winter's night nested in her heart. She doubts whether her spirit will ever again feel untroubled. She'd breathed a few prayers over the poor soul's grave, lighted a candle, its wick steadied and wavered as an orange teardrop, until the gentlest touch of a breeze snuffed it dead; and its little pang of smoke carried bitterness to her nostrils.

Dennis hasn't spoken to her since yesterday, not even to the children. His father had received a grunt in response to a question he'd asked about something or other.

Finally, he rolls off his tongue, "Elizabeth, you were right in everything you told me."

Still, he can't bring himself to look me in the eye, she thinks.

Elizabeth says, "A harmless man and his daughter butchered, and their house ruined and pilfered – for what, Dennis, how does that sort of thing do anyone any good?"

His voice downcast as he says, "Nellie is gone to Naas with Louise – I sent them up in one of the farm carts, with an escort for part of the way."

Aren't you the great man?

"She'll not survive," Elizabeth says, "little Louise, the wretched state of her. Did you see her – what was done."

Silence.

Elizabeth says, firmly, "Answer me."

"Yes."

"Twelve years old, Dennis, and full of deep cuts and slashes put in her by grown men."

"Those men will be dealt with; have no doubt."

"By whom – you? Are you the General now, is that it?"

"There's no need for that sort of guff."

"You'll all be dealt with. The whole bleddy lot of ye."

"Roger is-"

"Don't you dare mention that cur's name in my presence."

"Errah hush, will you. We have something in mind."

"Not with your two heads beaten together would ye have a bright mind. Fools, the pair of ye and those like ye."

Her stomach turns queasy and memories of the burial, the images, pain her. She watches him clasp his hands to his head, his eyes to the window.

"You won't find that bitch Hannah McGarry out there," she says. *Now, what has he got to say?*

*

Louise draws her last breath in front of her very eyes, a long and wheezing farewell, her small body has the slightest of quakes, then a silence in which all falls silent – Nellie feels as though her insides have turned to mush.

They had reached Naas an hour ago and were in the house of George's first cousin, a woman whom Nellie didn't much like – but in a crisis, family is family. And Andrea was admirably playing her part, helped of course by the deplorable sight of her niece and by the tales of the atrocity Nellie had related. *She's so like George in looks.*

George.

She cannot accept that he has gone from her forever. The two people in this world whom she'd dearly loved and had lived her life for, cruelly taken, leaving her without purpose for the days ahead. The past is my future for the rest of my days, she believes – the past accompanies you in the future, each as inseparable twins.

Shouldn't I feel worse than this? She asks herself in the kitchen, sitting quietly by the empty fireplace, as the undertakers set to putting her granddaughter into a coffin. She had smelt its fresh pine when they'd brought it in. Louise is in that other room with its paintings of river and woodland scenes. A thick musty smell pervades. Tiny fingers cling to her favourite cloth doll, blood stained, missing an eye button, part of its chequered blue dress torn.

She toys with the locket George gifted her for their wedding anniversary. God, these items were so popular back then – when? Oh, 1784 or was 1786 – hmm. How long were we married? A long time…I never really liked it, but what could I say? It was expensive. George mentioned the price of every present he bought for me, as though he felt it entirely necessary that my knowing would make me appreciate it all the more – never understanding that it was the little things he did, that cost him nothing which made me value him above everything money could buy. He said, "…and darling, remember the piece I read to you from the newspaper, about Prince George, sending the miniature painting of his *Eye* to Maria Fitzherbert…" She certainly remembered and also the scandal created by the prince's relationship with a widowed Catholic… though I wore it; had to so as not to hurt George. He sulked at times, for lengthy periods, if he felt strongly slighted. Nellie recalled telling her mother she hated the blooming thing…it resembled a glassy and bleary old eye, and God, its dangling around her neck…

so diminished her confidence, no matter how beautiful her dress.

Well, she can do what she likes with the object now. George's joking about, if he predeceased her, being able to keep an eye on her had grown so tiresome – well she'll keep it, but it'll remain in the little wooden jewellery box with other items of jewellery for which her own 'eye' had lost its taste.

Late afternoon, when the sun has gone off the boil, Nellie sets out for Dublin to bring her granddaughter home to her parents. Andrea had dispatched a horse rider in advance to advise the couple of the terrible calamity, insisting that Nellie should be spared having to personally deliver such tragic news.

She has not spoken at all on the 30-mile journey, not even responding to the driver's quietly spoken questions and observations, all primed with care so as not to cause her further anguish. He seems to find it necessary to console her by saying clichés: her suffering is over; we have to face into it ourselves; those rebels will burn in bleddy hell; Hell won't be hot enough for them. In the end Collins gives up and looks straight ahead. The skies are almost wrung out of daylight.

On the capital's approach road yeomanry search everyone entering and leaving the city. When a sergeant approaches Collins the driver says, "Sur, we have a grieving woman here and a dead child there in the back. Murdered by the Kildare rebels."

"Is that so?"

At his doubting tone, Nellie lifts her chin "I beg your pardon?"

The sergeant turns to the men behind him, "Open the coffin."

Collins protests, "Ah now, Sur."

Nellie says, "This is an outrage. How dare you defile…"

The sergeant shakes his head apologetically and says, "I have my orders – the rebels are moving weapons into the city using coffins and later digging them up in the graveyards –

I'm truly sorry, Ma'am. I have my orders…"

Is there nothing the insurgents will not stoop to, nor a depth where we will not follow them? Nellie asks herself.

She hears the dragging of the coffin, the prising open of its lid, nails squeaking like caught mice, the horrified gasps from the men as they stare at Louise and the extent of her injuries. They fix the lid as quickly as possible – there is its return drag along the floor of the cart.

She says nothing to the sergeant's profuse apologies and condolences. What she does respond to is his promise that her daughter's death would be avenged, to rely on the crown forces to give her that measure of succour. *My daughter?*

A smile almost escapes her.

"Yes,' she agrees, "it is what keeps me going, the solid belief that justice will be done."

*

Duff puts his quill in the blue ceramic inkwell. Beads of perspiration moisten the pages and runs the ink in a couple of places. He goes outside and holds it up to the sun to dry. He reads…

'Your Lordship:

Our forced march has brought us to an advanced position; am approaching Kildare with seven pieces of artillery, 150 dragoons and 650 infantry, determined to make a dreadful example of the rebels.'

*

Life before this, Elizabeth considers, was much better if hard, and because of this… this…she can find in her no words to describe the mayhem; it is going to become even more difficult. They will have to endure trials more severe and testing than those which had prompted rebellion – these notions are vines tangling around her throat, tightening.

Another scorcher. In less than an hour the sun will be at its highest. She, along with Jack and Sally, look on as the men march out of the town, not in orderly fashion as the militia had done, but as a raggle-taggle outfit, talking and laughing among themselves, leaving nothing in their wake except a town full of women and children (though some had left too, she'd gathered, and were hiding out in the basement of a large house a mile out the road).

People begin to slowly disperse, like autumn leaves in a lazy breeze, returning to their main street cottages, to await whatever the day unfolds. These are people who had done nothing untoward, did not agree with or abet the rising, from the outset had seen the folly…snippets she had overheard and yet Elizabeth knows for sure that a few of these women and children had cheered while watching a man's death throes.

The dust settles with the silence.

Always an itch in him to be away from us, Elizabeth ponders as she watches Dennis. Even the horse has it, scratching at the ground with its left hoof. Flies swarm about its tail.

"You may join your *men*, so," she says.

He rubs his lips, then Jack's shock of hair, rests his hand on his shoulder. Sun burned cheeks and foreheads, and the skin peeling on their arms. The spit of each other.

"If I want to get the protection notice," he says.

"Hmm."

"What? You don't want me to get it now?" he says, with an exasperated shake of his head.

Young Jack asks, "Can I go?"

Sally gasps, "Don't be a fool, you."

Elizabeth says in a hard tone, "Run along home and check on your grandfather – he's not well."

"I-" Jack begins.

Dennis says, "Do as your mother says."

Jack's chin drops but he catches the mood and realises there is no point in protesting – besides his grandfather really isn't well; his knees yawn creaks, his eyes miss much, he talks nonsense about stuff people aren't interested in and he sees people who are dead. Tells Mother so and so was dead, and the next day Mother spotted the dead woman very much alive.

The two children cross the road, Sally giving a little skip behind her brother.

Elizabeth confides, "I have a bad feeling about this, Dennis. I feel that the protection letter will serve only one use, to wipe your arse."

Father Farrell, Elizabeth notices, is making his way over to them, emerging from the laneway, his hands behind his back. It is a natural trajectory, this route. He is not going out of his way to see them. A rotund man, fond of his whiskey but not to the extent where he allows it to master his tongue. A Carmelite from the Whitelands he had pleaded with the likes of Dennis and McGarry to seek out a peaceful solution. As he draws nearer, she sees the smile, like a lifting of cloud from the path of the sun. His big hands join in a loud clap.

"All over bar the shouting,' he says, "thanks be to God."

Dennis says gruffly, "I'll be on my way,' having small time for the priest, knowing that if the clergy in its entirety had called the population to arms the country might have stood together and gained independence – they'd argued that changes were happening, Catholics could buy land, do this and that – and yes it was true. But who are the English and Irish English to bestow our natural rights – this is not their country, Dennis believes.

The priest says, "Good now, isn't it – that all this killing and defiling the countryside is going to stop – I saw myself now, only yesterday, ten rotting cattle left behind by the United Irishmen camp – an army marches on its belly, but they left behind much good meat to go bad. Such a waste of human life too, corpses…" he falls silent.

Elizabeth says, after Dennis has mounted, "Be careful, Dennis."

"I'll see you later this evening."

There follow moments of silence that the priest feels he should fill, "Indeed he will of course, Elizabeth…for sure. With the help of almighty God.'

*

Although she had not brought the shocking news to Patrick, her son, and Ann Marie, she may as well have done for upon seeing her each went into such a dreadful state. And this before they had laid eyes on their poor daughter who at this very moment the undertaker is trying to make presentable for viewing.

"There was nothing I could do to save them…George, I couldn't persuade him to leave sooner…" she says in the drawing room, much later, after telling people about the tragedy for the umpteenth time. A pressman from *Freemans Journal* said he would write a damning piece – the whole kingdom will learn of the barbarity of this action. Callous. He'd said this several times in different modulations, as though juggling the variations.

Several hot cognacs fail to warm her blood. People are kindly toward her: she had lost a husband and a granddaughter, but she feels guilty for having survived and she tells the pastor it is wrong of God to let an old woman live and a child die – she would swap places with Louise in an instant.

The pastor, after just viewing Louise's remains, sits his words behind his blanched expression, remains silent. There is no more solace left in him; he has spoken it all, and then when he finds the silence too heavy to hold, says "…we take solaces wherever and whenever we find them and pray in hope."

"Patrick," she says abruptly, and she would have called for Ann Marie too, but the family doctor has sedated her daughter in-law, for her wails and shrieks had upset people.

Her son hurries to her and takes her hand, "Mother."

"I'm so sorry…"

Like the pastor, he too cannot find words of impact.

*

Sally picks up the rumour from Mrs Kelly and carries it home, just ahead of Jack who butts in as his sister commences to elaborate. The two children begin to bicker. Elizabeth says, putting away the bellows and looking into the fire, "Stop! One at a time. Sally…"

"Ah-" Jack says.

"Shush with you, go on Sally."

Sally breathes in deeply, trying to remember verbatim what old Mrs Kelly had said,

"Mammy, she said Lord Roden's Foxhunters were in a riotous and drunken brawl on Claregate street last night, carrying articles of rebel apparel on the top of their fixed bayonets, and swearing most vehemently, 'We are the boys who will slaughter the croppies tomorrow at the Curragh.'

Elizabeth reflects for moments before saying, "I am sure that was all drink talk for why would a difference be made between one go of rebels in Kilcullen and another in Kildare?"

"Perhaps we should warn Father," Sally says.

'Let me go,' Jack says.

"Tell me what else you heard?" Elizabeth says.

"Samuel Cannington and his Suffolks' are coming this way."

Cannington? Elizabeth thinks. Everything is happening very quickly, as if the days want to become the past in a hurry…as one would wish away the time spent in labour.

The cat throws itself under the fireplace as though it is trying itself out to become a rug…rolls over on his tummy, "Aren't you getting a fat boy, altogether."

*

The moro has all the makings of a bad day and no chance of change overnight, McGarry's gut speaks. He feels sick to the pit of his stomach – the tip of his left small finger aches – if someone had complained of this pain to him, he would have thought the man hardly one at all – but by Christ, this hurt grieves him so. Perhaps a legacy from Monasterevin, when he'd received a blow to his neck from Henderson the yeoman. *Bad cur that fella. Only for young Carty saw the bastard off; I'd be a dead man.* His neck has bothered him since…the calling of the gibbet?

*

This rath with its high grassy embankment and deep trench and central flat circular swathe, is a long-forsaken homestead of the O'Toole clan, driven to the mountains by the Normans. Older than the Star of Bethlehem by a great many years, McGarry believes. Now, and for the last while, it is somewhere for the King's troops to hang rapparees and united Irishmen. He does not like the mood of the undulating plain of golden furze and tall thistles, its meandering sheep in search of a full trough and scrawny foxes, too; he has a particular dislike for those, for no reason. I am out of rope, words a hangman will never utter – we ourselves would say we've run out of road, but wouldn't believe twas true – that is where I am.

A brassy sun, short grass cropped above stiffened ground, furze shiny-coined petals, the meaty aroma from blazing campfires, idle chatter from those sitting around them, a great spreading by thousands of voices, half as many that had attended the Beatitude's loaves and fishes, blathering – some decent people, others pure braggards, in attire of all sorts, most of it ill-fitting, the working dun petalled with green cockades, features of militia and yeomanry uniform, pikes locking horns in conical stacks, flintlocks tucked against waistlines, swords sheathed, mostly prised from a dead yeoman's rigor mortis grip.

Not a breeze harries the air this morning…making available to nostrils the stench of melting horse dung, the clarity of yammering sheep prior to the blade, the buzzing of bluebottles, the off key singing of a ballad by a red-faced man too drunk to hold his feet to the grass, a screeching laughter from a woman known to laugh at little funny or unfunny, or at another's misfortune, is followed by a blaze of curses against a woman who'd dipped her finger in her nose and drew a beacon of snot, wiping it in her mauve skirt.

Nearing his destination, the rath location of his own troop. Dundas, indeed,…just because the devil's chosen not to show his horns; it doesn't follow that you should smile at him. Same with the fellow coming to see us tomorrow from the town below, down there no doubt stuffing himself under the long shadow of the round tower, debating with himself how he should handle us, and only I know of him, who he is, what we did to one blood of his, I would be stuck here in the moro, waiting for what is coming. A thistle waiting for the scythe.

It fails to register with others, this young officer on his way to enlist with his uncle…though they stood beside me when we questioned him. Am I the only one who had heard him mention his uncle's name? Duff.

Saluting certain of the men, one wants his ear, asks if he knows what the bleddy hell is going on. There are more turns than a liar's tongue. Roger smiles, shrugs, and again, as he says, "Gerry, if you have a need to visit home, then head there, but Kildare I warn you is not the direction you should make toward."

"I live there."

'No, you live here. Where you lived doesn't exist, not anymore.'

The man stares hard at McGarry, eyes glazed, as though a fire has caught behind them. McGarry waves at a subordinate and joins him when beckoned to a campfire.

After a call to air a ballad taught to him by his father, McGarry slips away from the main campfire nursing a rum bottle underarm, laughing, saying he wouldn't trust his companions not to drink it in his absence. But he is not as drunk as they believe, as he feigns stumbling, past…

Blunderbuss's, muskets, flintlocks, sabres, pike heads, pike staffs, assembled pikes stacked and piles of them lying atop the other, criss-crossing and rising as though in some maddening pattern of knitwork, alongside them small knolls of other weapons crudely fashioned, farm tools, scythes and spears even…the noise of things falling was not deafening, they fell, he had been informed, with the empty din of resignation, which is louder.

800 pikes had been found at Monasterevin and less than 20 firearms, all abandoned by our lads as they fled the field, McGarry

thought, gathering what his young bodyguard had told him, the boyo with the quiet mouth and good hearing, a fella who'd banished talking out his thoughts, and took all in, netting lies, distortions and truths, unable to tell one from the other. A clear-eyed and steady shot, a wildfowler like his late father, the smithy thought to have been murdered by the womenfolk in his house. A pleasant man in company, I had always thought. A master wrought-iron maker.

"Deo Deora," he mutters, walking on, tears of Christ, indeed.

A tiredness burdens him, a tiredness he tries to lose in his bedspace in the furze.

Tired enough to sleep but oblivion is locked on the horizon, and the weariness moves sluggishly through his veins as river debris. The day aged before its time, he senses. Each moment drags…

What we know but chose to ignore because it is out of sight, is that the redcoats' gibbets are waiting. Duff moves nowhere without them. Ready and waiting as a hawk with his eye on a prey, lingering in the sky until the moment of dive.

The quickest to turn about face on a promise is a king's man. And Duff is the quickest of them. A man who prays in church is oft the one who preys on folk.

Dare I tell anyone of this gut feeling? Ardently speak? I would like to appraise Downey but the man has a sod of turf for a brain. A decent enough fella with a weakness for Hannah – God, now – sister that she is, she's nothing more than a large pain in any man's pincushion, too many heads on her coin to be trusted. Told me much about the king's men for a couple of pence.

If I had four good men with silent tongues, we could do a service…and visit Duff where he bivvies. An assassination would leave a message; they are no longer safe in their beds. For sure if we were successful, the blade of vengeance would wreak, but among us there not that many with stealthy tongues…so the notion hangs like a spent pecker.

We are done. All of my notions bleach at the bottom of the barrel.

Good man that Downey but he makes the wrong choice on too many occasions; is too shame-faced to ever get away with doing much of what he knows is wrong.

A gibbous moon in a clear sky, the softest of breezes, starry specks. No doubt our last gathering as an army. Time now to be stealthy. That fella Duff – if he bloody reincarnates it'll be as a stone…his heart is buried in his arse.

Boots has left for Kilcullen in a dash to have Dundas rein in his fellow officer, to query if his lordship's detail are present with Duff, to administer the handing over, as he had promised Reverend Shannon. I think it a sign that thus far there is no sign. I know Boots as well as I know my own dark side. Dark sides…tis everyone has one, but most believe we don't need anything to come our way that carries the sting of a curse, so we keep matters in check best we can. My thoughts are like wind swirled dust; they can settle nowhere.

Tis time to settle some dust somewhere.

The devil's bugle sounds tomorrow.

I know this…it's the last blow of the hammer that had fastened my thoughts. No one here has thought to broach Kildare ferrying a white flag, to parlay with Duff.

Duff is no Dundas; they know this at least…I think.

Since arriving here, he has been planning to steal away unnoticed and make for the Bog of Allen some 16 miles distant. It is the only sure safe place left. No cavalry could make it across the wetlands, slipping and sliding and sinking in feculent bog, nor would infantry prevail in its vast expanse. A man could live secure in that natural fortress, if he had enough supplies to see out the patience of those waiting to ensnare him beyond the frontiers of the bog. A game where chess piece moves are slowly contrived and maddeningly considered.

It would be rough living, but McGarry is sure he will not be alone. A few rapparees whom he knows have hideouts there. He owns enough coinage to soften their way.

Sparks rise and crackle from a freshened fire, and wood smoke blights the air. Nearby a man coughs hard, another passes by him without a word kind, but a loud belch.

He walks past a line of tethered horses, saying to Ted, “How’s my lad?”

“Fine, Captain.”

“As soon as I relieve myself, we’ll be off, so follow me along to the furze with our three horses and go easy with the noise.”

“Captain.”

His eyes are on the stars. A clear night sky holds promise of a good day. The moro, he is almost certain, will yield disaster. Guilt runs through him as a weeping sore. He has fought against himself, to keep this realisation in his head, convinced that none would believe him – most likely they would dismiss his concerns, not act on them and decamp. Granted, there is the slimmest of hope they would do otherwise, but he strongly believes it is too slender to be described as such.

One does well now to look out for himself and himself alone.

*

Reverend James Shannon

I can hardly refuse these hard-faced fellows, McGarry who I did not know and Downey with whom I only had a nodding acquaintance. Their proposition that I serve as an arbitrator for the insurgents camped on the plains, during their negotiations with Lord Dundas, appeared ludicrous. They said it would benefit them to have a Protestant clergyman from Kildare lending his voice to and recommending their terms and conditions to one of his own faith. An officer who'd signed the terms with the Kilcullen rebels at Knockaulin Hill. Perhaps, so. It is difficult for me not to imagine the gross deaths of poor Crawford, the wounds inflicted upon his charming granddaughter, of the dreadful hanging of Meaney in the Market Square. Of Duncan Smith who'd arrived at my door with two pike thrusts to his back, bleeding to death on the kitchen table; a more agonising death I had never previously witnessed.

I left with them almost immediately, bringing my Bible, a tobacco pouch and a winter coat because Curragh breezes can chill the very marrow. I rode with them to their camp, and from there the intention was that I journey to Kilcullen with other rebel officers to negotiate terms of surrender, to procure a promise of a letter guaranteeing safety for those surrendering their arms, and I confess it made my insides queasy to think that men and women who had committed heinous crimes would walk free from their wrong doings. For the greater good, I suppose; hadn't Lord Dundas's clemency brought Kilcullen and districts a return to at least a version of tranquillity?

The camp at Gibbet Rath.

I am among the mass, just. Passing through.

There are those who peg blankets together and drape them over a rope knotted to stakes, fashioning bivouacs. More sleep under the stars, huddled close to campfires, stoking the embers before adding fuel, because nighttime yields a heavy dew and a bone chill.

The hills northwest of the encampment range as dark brooding shadows. The air stinks with the acridity of burning peat, pipe smoke, unwashed bodies and clothes, dried and fresh perspiration, urine and animal faeces – the mildest of breezes rises and carries, caressing the grassy terrain with the cooling sigh of something undefined but redolent of a dying man's closing breath, there, present, but going and in the end quickly gone. The last shivering of the darkening left to the spiny thorn and its quivering gold petals, not too unlike the final lowering of the yellow harp on the field of surrender and submission and yet, purportedly lifesaving.

They drink hard liquor, too much, too frequently, to blank the images of their campaigns for freedom – things done to them, that they did to others. They want to forget and nothing else settles their minds, for a while, only alcohol – it also blankets fear. Fear of dying in the way they'd witnessed their comrades and enemies dying, of not seeing another 'moro, or their families, of never again wakening to the sound of birdsong, of never being able to fill that desolate hollow deep within themselves.

McGarry talks. He speaks over tea, which I suspect is not usual for him. Tea. I believe he knows where his head should be in crucial times. He is a furtive man, alert, always present but looking elsewhere, I sense, whilst Downey's features speak of a man enduring great stress, addled with indecisiveness, of having no idea of where to turn, of a man expecting the worse to happen… they talk of their gladness to see the business over; their regret at how things had played out, the harm it did, but mention too their disappointments at their failure to achieve freedom, the societal freedom where all are treated as all, equal. It is then, I see them as complete fools, for the world has never been an equal place, nor will it ever be – unless God wills it; war and murder and mayhem will strike everything except an even balance.

After returning from Kilcullen, and forwarding a militia despatch rider to General Duff, carrying a stamped letter from Lord Dundas, O'Byrne reneges on his promise to allow me to return to my house. He says I can keep the Catholic priest company … indeed. Good man that Father Farrell is, I would sooner be off this cursed hill. O'Byrne too worries, for Duff has not sent a reply, and Dundas hasn't, McGarry says, as yet, detailed a party to assist Duff in overseeing the surrendering of arms. How would he know of this? That man is a watcher. A watcher is one who sees what others fail to notice.

*

From the darkness, the silhouette of a man framed by the orange of flames, speaks,

"Where are you off to?" Dennis says.

McGarry turns slowly, bottle under his arm, fixing his breeches.

"Ah, the hard man Dennis."

"I overheard you telling Ted Carty to bring three horses along."

"You did; indeed. It's what I said."

"So?"

McGarry sighs, thinks of his satchels and other bric-a-brac in the furze; they contain food supplies, his tobacco, a spare clay pipe, a flintlock pistol with a can of powder and some cleaning rods, ammunition, blankets, narrow rolls of hessian, rope, an axe, sharp knives, tentage. Necessities for survival in the wilderness.

"You're deserting us," Dennis says without reproach.

"Am I. Indeed. Deserting what exactly?"

"Why? The protection notice – I don't understand. You will not survive without it."

McGarry says, "Perhaps I have a bad feeling about tomorrow, Dennis, perhaps a little bird has whispered something in my ear. Can you not feel the tension in the air?"

Dennis says, "What knowledge have you?"

"That Gifford was Duff's nephew and that if I were him, I would want to drown the plains in Popish blood. You remember the boy – at the mail coach?"

"Yes, Christ. He died in a terrible way."

'Listen, I hear it – I smell it – they wouldn't give us the notices on Knockaulin – they used a good excuse for a bad purpose. Now, Dundas has promised but not moved a leg on it..."

McGarry feels something give in the other, as though the earth has shaken under his feet and he is questioning if the experience has been real.

"Jesus," Dennis mutters, massaging his neck as though the news had entered there.

"Ride with us, Dennis."

"No... no... no... I can't."

"Why not?"

"You must tell O'Byrne and-"

"He'd heed, do you imagine? You're a fool if you stay here – you've got a farm, a lovely wife, and my lovely sister-"

"Shut your face!"

"It's no secret – Hannah's a good woman but her legs are like her lips – she can't keep them together. She's worse than any man for it."

"I won't tell you again, Roger."

"Nor I, you."

There's a pause, like that of a twig breaking in the silence of a deep wood. McGarry then starts on Lord Edward, whom he had met once, of his walk from his fancy Kildare town residence across the Curragh with a friend – he wore a green silk cravat and when challenged by two dragoons demanding he remove it, he put it to them that he would not; but if they wanted to try and take it from him...well, they were welcome. He liked the man, respected him, except for the bottle green suit he was never going to wear. But…but…he had courage, had been injured on the battlefield out foreign, and was carried from the battle by a black man called Small. His lordship employed him…Small was a freeman, do you gather what I'm saying?

No, I take it, Dennis, you don't.

Small was a large man, black…my first one to see…a mighty powerful sight for the eyes, let me tell you. You'd nearly want to scrub him…lips plumper that Joey Harrington, a broken nose – broken more than once you could tell. And eyes like those of a noble steed. He stuck out from among the rest of us, a black chicklet, and he could not make sense of one thing about us…he said why in the name of all who are supposed to be watching down on us, did we allow ourselves to be corralled by people not worthy of that title – we are as stupid and naïve as his own kind, those stolen from Africa, as are the Indian tribes…for selling their ancient homelands for glass baubles. Here, the church says progress has been made – and so it has…

Dennis says, 'Look…'

"There's no look, this is our country not theirs, how dare they think it isn't ours. I could go on and on…But it's time I was off. What I'm trying to drum into your head, Dennis, is this…don't be stupid. Don't be naïve."

Horses clip-clop on the dew drenched grassland, one giving a little whinny.

"Grab a hauld of all of them things of ours, Ted," he whispers to the youth, who hands him the reins and disappears out of sight, dropping low into the mouth of furze.

"Now," McGarry says, "would you just this once, fall on the right side of good sense."

"We can't desert them…Reverend Shannon is here. He'll-"

"They won't heed his meek and croaky voice."

Harshly, irritated, McGarry adds "When things go wrong make for the Bog of Allen – remember I said it to you before, if the rebellion went badly. We can wildfowl and forage for our existence, until the smoke clears."

It does not take long for the youth to load up the dray horses, to mount up. McGarry follows suit and says as he grips the reins of the supply horse. "Drop those green cockades, lad…we don't need to be showing that side of ourselves. Not anymore."

Dennis says, "You should be shot."

"Spoken like a true officer. O'Byrne is after rubbing off on you."

"I-"

"They're below in that town, tonight…preparing for us. On a mad rip they are. If you go through this bunch of furze to the main road, up the road itself a wee bit, and raise your ear, you might hear their voices carrying. There's no peace in their words; I'll tell you that. They sound like a devil's bellowing."

"Duff is an officer – he'll obey his orders."

"Which are?"

'To accept our arms in surrender.'

"And you can't risk going home to that lovely wife of yours without a protection notice in your pocket. Sin a bhfuil – that's how it is. Take the caul from your eyes, man. Goddam it!"

He nudges his horse into motion, riding north. Dennis peers into the darkness, as though searching for a light, in the end thinking that he has long seen it go out.

*

Elizabeth compares her heart to a fractured vase lightly bound with thin smiles of horse glue; it'll never beat the same again. A sigh flees from the depth of her being – God…she so detests these broiling days – they have brought her nothing but trouble. Much prefer the song of a breeze, the harsh lashing of rain against the walls and roof of their home, to see frost on the grass, cobwebs like crystal art on hedgerows, tiny bird prints fossil like at feeding points. Bright as the day is, warm as it is, the day stinks of a curse – a bleddy cesspit full of the best stuff that marks the militia and yeomanry. The living live beside the dead. The dead live as the dead in the adjacent cemetery that is Elizabeth's neighbour, lying in wait for the resurrection at the end of all time. Franciscans once dwelt there, slept in their beehive cells, worshipped in their cross like designed stone church, worked the fields, until an English king commanded them to swear allegiance to him before Rome, therefore setting himself as a god. The cells reveal their locations under grass hillocks; dense ivy shrouds those church walls left standing, upper recesses indicate where flooring was secured. Garlic flourishes among the ancient slab markers, details lichened and weathered and timeworn…occasionally she catches the faint aroma of garlic, hears the whisperings of the old oaks, their creaking limbs during storms, a splintering of wood in the harshest of winds – once she had espied a fox cub asleep under a leaning headstone, and another time witnessed a badger emerging from its lair, a grave with a rusty iron cross looped by a rustier circle. Members of the Fitzgeralds are buried there, exact locations unknown…the uncrowned Kings of Ireland… she mutters.

Dennis's family are not buried there. Neither are hers. His lineage are buried in the acres that flow from the cathedral grounds, under the watchful round tower, but he wants, whenever he passes, to be buried with his mother's side in Lackagh, near where St Bridget's father is said to have lived, a few miles outside of town.

Why am I thinking like this? It's over. He will show tomorrow with the protection order and they can get back on with their lives, living beside the dead; until it is their time for the great waiting to finish in grand old age.

*

He spends the evening in a coffee house on the market square with his officers. He is unusually quiet and remote from the conversation, interacting enough for the sake of politeness.

There is a situation of some gravity aching within him. A dispatch he had earlier received from Dundas to the effect that 3,000 rebels had accepted terms of amnesty, that a sizeable quantity of arms and ammunition had been handed over at Old Kilcullen. Pikes and guns were stacked higher than the treasury at the Royal Exchange…they behaved sensibly and were allowed disperse to their homes…the hills did not run with blood.

The rebellion in Kildare has ended. Extend the same conditions to the rebels in Kildare.

The man had some nerve. A weak fellow. Such generous terms to a people who had raped, murdered and plundered. Betrayed the King.

Dundas is a coward. Afraid of meting justice to the belligerents for fear of administrative consequence. Loyalty to the crown is first and foremost – the first port of call for body and soul. Justice naturally follows this tenet. A fool.

A voice extracts him from the well of his thoughts, "Sir, there are some 4,000 rebels gathered on the plains, according to the latest reports."

"And, Captain Cannington, tell me your regards of that tally?"

Cannington said, "It could be much shy of being accurate. Perhaps 2,000. A little over or under."

"What would you propose?"

"Sir?"

Duff pans the length of the table and then staring at Cannington he says, "I'm asking you for your suggestion – if you were to oversee the field tomorrow, what would you do?"

"Accept their surrender."

"What makes you say that?"

"Lord Dundas's actions, Sir, has taken many rebels out of the fray."

"They're never taken out until they are dead, you understand."

Cannington nods, and says, "Sir, if I may…"

Duff gestures.

"Fitzgerald said of us that what we have we hold, what we want we take…they see us on their land, still. Land stolen from them. This is what we have to deal with, we cannot erase the past unless-"

"Stop there. Unless you mean to say until they are dead."

Cannington, cowed by his senior officer and the glares of others seated around the table, "Until as you say, Sir."

'Hmm. No. I think a cavalry charge might be a better alternative.'

"They are to surrender to us,' Cannington says, uncertain as to what he should have said.

There are ripples of disapproval and tut-tutting from his fellow officers.

"Meaning?" Duff says.

"Dundas – General Lake…"

"I have read no such order, heard none of it – if the rebels wish to lay down their arms, then we will accept their surrender. Let us pray this will be what they want."

Duff stands and waves those at the table to remain seated and says, "The morning comes early. Gentlemen – do not delay too long to retire after my departure."

*

After looking in on her children and their grandfather in the stone barn, she returns to the main house to fetch hard-boiled eggs and a loaf for their breakfast. It is late at night and she hopes the house would be asleep – her home is full of free quarterers, the King's troops eating and drinking their fill of their hosts' limited resources. Unlike others she'd heard of, these weren't lewd or loud men, most likely kept quiet by Cannington.

Ensconced in her kitchen are four Fencibles, and a couple of the town's loose women, including your one Hannah, sitting on a soldier's knee as though it is a horse.

"The good woman herself," Cannington says by way of greeting.

He is drunk. So much for his keeping things sound.

"I've come in here for some food."

"Stay," he says.

"No."

Hannah says, "She can't – she's saving it for her husband, Dennis – he's out on the plains there praying for his life, for the biteen of paper."

Cannington says quickly, calmly, alertly "Is that so, Elizabeth?"

"Yes."

"You never said anything to me about this."

He likes her. Elizabeth knows. She likes him, too. It would never lead to anything for he is a good deal younger, by about eight years, and what had happened between them had happened a long time ago in the Cannington household when she had been a maid there.

Hannah goes to speak but he scolds her to silence. Unsteadily, he gets to his feet and follows Elizabeth into the scullery.

She wraps eggs and slices of a brown loaf in a cloth.

"You need to get word to him – to get the blazes out of there."

He crosses his lips with his forefinger, slaps the wall, and returns to the kitchen.

She is rooted to the spot, as though her bare feet had been planted in a bed of nettles.

*

McGarry is aware the militia are encamped at many of the small raths on the plains, to prevent the rebels from pursuing the course of action he'd embarked upon.

Knowing the terrain well, and because their campfires served as warning signs, he easily circumvents them. Leaving the Curragh behind, they keep to the farmlands, avoiding the roads and encroach the edges of the bog just as daylight begins to edge through.

Almost safe now, he thinks, nursing his horse past a derelict cottage, its roof caved in, hearth strong and sturdy, firewalls soot blackened. Scorched grass spout from its chimney, a tracery of poppies in a backyard along with tall thistles and nettlebeds, daisies, buttercups, violets...

His grandparents' home lost to the family because of a rent driven too high by an unscrupulous landlord. A man into whose head he had put a ball at Clane and felt 1,000 times better for it; but it wasn't long before the feeling turned to lard in his belly.

What you think might you make feel good in yourself isn't often lasting.

Ahead, lay an abundance of purple heather. Moss, too. The commingled smell as familiar to him as the smoke from his forge.

He stops. His horse shakes its head, ninnies, then falls still.

Listens to the birdsong. Observes a robin, two, on a branch. A good omen.

Carty says, 'What's the matter?'

"Nothing, nothing…let's kick on, into the midst of where our breaths are safest."

A picture of a place, he thinks, despite the midges, the flies, the exposure to the elements, only a copse of wood here and there, not good land for a man with a weak deposition – a cough would worsen and a soughing wind could bring on a clinging melancholy. There are murder victims sown hereabouts, sealed up in the boggy earth, bodies down the centuries, whose spirits haunt the bogs at night, force cracks in people's minds, who cry for justice in a land devoid of any…this is no fair world.

Sinkholes, he remembers have sucked cottages, man and animals downward within an instant. There are parts hereabout where the bogland's heart is pure mulch, lying in deadly wait for a person's misstep…it happens to those who don't know the terrain, and those who forget.

Suddenly. as though he'd fallen into a well of despondency, Carty says with a tremor, "This is not for me."

"It is, for now, lad," McGarry sighs deeply, "hold your nerve."

"I'll leave you the horse. I'll go by foot."

"Where to, exactly?"

"Home."

"You'll be strung up before the day's over. They saw you, boy – they saw us. Do you understand what I'm saying? How many men have you killed?"

"Three. Maybe five."

"Stay with me – we'll see this out. I promised your mother you would be okay. I've failed in all else I've set out to do, don't let me fail here. I have a wife too and a son your age…I can't go to them either. We must wait this out."

Tears well in the boy's eyes, the mildest of shudders in the flesh of his jaw.

"We can only roll it forward lad, if we're lucky to get a chance to do that. I'm talking about time. Once it's spent, it's spent…let's head now, no more guff."

"Okay."

"Sursum Corda, Ted, eh?"

"What does that mean?"

"Did you ever go to Mass and not fall asleep – it's Latin for lift up your hearts…"

"You know Latin?"

"I listened to a priest for a time in my life."

They ride on, making for the wildwood and beyond it to the hide in the bulrushes.

His saddle bag is lumpy with coin…thinks on three chestnut horses grazing in a field of buttercups, a wealthy man's creatures, safe from pillage, having bought protection for his place and his family. Neither sin nor harm done in milking him hard once more. Yesterday's visit had proved worthwhile. What the rich have they hold, what they want, they take…no matter how much we take from them, twill never come near the measure of what they have taken from us.

*

"I'll go," Dennis's father said, old Brian.

"With your bent back and your limp, you'll never get there in time," she says.

"It's only five fields away."

Lifting his head from the pillow Jack says, "I'll go with him,"

"Shush," Elizabeth smothers.

"You're needed here, Elizabeth," the old man insists, "to keep an eye on the house, and Sally too – you know what the dragoons are like – there's a bad cut to one or two of them where children are concerned."

"Why can't you mind her?'

'With my bad back and terrible knee?' he says, smiles. "And I think they fear you more than me, too. Let me tarry – they're less likely to harm an old man."

She considers. The encampment is as the crow flies takes about 20 minutes, an hour if they went via the town, and they wouldn't be allowed to proceed beyond the yeomanry toll post – even trying to would most likely bring a heap of trouble down on their heads.

"Right so," she says, unsure if she is doing the right thing.

In truth, she is heart sickened of Dennis and his carry-on. How thick he is to get through to and she'd seen something else too – Hannah is in her house now and her tongue has an itch to whiplash the bitch.

That common tramp is spitting silent news at her. Sharp biteens, with relish.

*

It isn't safe for Mrs Crawford to return home. Not now, the officer had said. But the time is rapidly approaching when she would be able to, if that is what she wants.

Of course, it is what she craves. Kildare is her home, where she'd been born, lived and raised. Married. Gave birth. It is where she will die.

Ann Marie says, halting her knitting, "Nellie, you can stay with us…Patrick wants you to. I do."

"I have failed you and my son miserably – I wish I had died along with Louise and George. I wish I were dead and to know nothing."

Patrick says, turning from the bay window, pinching at the corner of his moustache, "Don't be saying such things, Mother."

"Patrick, I *will* be going home. I'll be doing as the minister advised, drawing up an inventory of what items have been stolen from my home, the damage caused – it will all be replaced, and the home renovated. By not going back, they'll think they'll have won something. Besides, it's where I expect I'll feel nearest to George and Louise. And I also have some business to sort out."

"Who are *they*?" Patrick queries, sitting to the armrest of his wife's rose-patterned armchair.

"The townspeople – the good and the bad of them, who else, Patrick? The very ones who stood by and let this happen."

"That woman," Ann Marie says bitterly.

Nellie does not reply to this oblique reference to her house servant, Hannah.

*

After losing sight of McGarry, Dennis re-joins the group, sitting beside O'Byrne. Art is merry – the whole camp is in a jovial mood. Banter, laughter, a calmness, too. Men spread in groups, tending to turf fires, talking, swapping tales. Reminiscing. He thinks it redolent of the loaves and the fishes…all the hungry people waiting. Where are McGarry's worries, his concerns? They are not present here. *All I see are people happy and eager for all this madness to be over.*

"You're quiet in yourself," Art notices, passing the jug to Dennis.

"McGarry has taken his leave of us," Dennis says, no longer able to contain himself.

Anger rises in O'Byrne. He calls for Tiernan and when Boots arrives, he instructs Dennis to repeat what he had just said.

Tiernan listens and says, "You let him go."

"I watched him," Dennis says, "yes. I consider it his loss, I..."

"A bad craythur," Art says, "the man was never any good, I always said it of him. He is too hidden – what goes on in that head of his I would not like to know."

"I don't understand," Tiernan says, "he needs the protection notice. We all do."

"Perhaps, he doesn't think Duff will give us our notices or Dundas will send his men,"

Dennis says, taking a quaff.

Next, he informs them why he might not.

Tiernan is first to speak, nervously, conspiratorially. "We should keep this to ourselves."

Art says with a quiver in his tone, "We cannot delay here another moment."

Dennis says, "What...we can't simply abandon-"

"Abandon, no – we must get word to Dundas, to explain our fears to him, to ask him to come and for himself to oversee the handing over. Demand it of him."

"I'll venture there again," Tiernan says, "I'll take two men with me and make haste."

Art and Dennis nod slowly.

"Ride quickly, Boots," Art says, "daylight will soon nibble away the night – don't leave us with hanging hands, not knowing how we should act."

Confidence reaches higher ground, after the act of something being done. Should the army break camp and make for Kilcullen, is a drifting thought, parley with Dundas himself?

Dennis slugs from the jug, wipes his lips with the back of his hand, irritating a cold sore. A good decision by O'Byrne. Dundas is a man of his word; he won't stand idly by and allow Duff to besmirch what is, after all, a gentleman's agreement.

*

She waits for an opportunity. At last candlelight dies in the upper rooms, and she hears the talk tether to silence in the kitchen and prays for the slut to come out for ablutions. A couple of the women had done so already and some men; left the house and went to the wooden privy. They'll do this for she'd told Sally not to empty the chamber pots. Lazy swine, those folk. From behind the apple tree she'd watched them unsteadily wend their way; one sang a song, another coughed, all made noises of sorts to let the rats know of their coming and going.

There. She is.

Prayers answered.

The last to empty herself.

Elizabeth hurries towards the privy door, approaching Hannah side-on, as she lifts its latch and whispers, "Say it to my face, now that you have no one to belittle me in front of."

"Oh, it's yourself," Hannah says, turning to face Elizabeth, startled.

The stench from the outhouse, no worse than the cesspit at the abbey boundary wall, is overpowering – never intended for so much use. It will be moved in time, after the shite dragoons have gone.

"How well do you really know my husband?"

"I just know him."

"How well?"

Silence.

Elizabeth says, "We women – we must strive to keep things out in the open with each other, don't you agree?"

"If you say so."

"You'll be just putting a stamp to what I already know."

Hannah sighs. She is torn but only marginally and she replies, "Yes. In the ways you think, I know of him."

Elizabeth feels a wrench, a tilting of something deep within her.

"Now what do I say if your husband asks me about you and Samuel Cannington – and I'm sure he will…after I drop a hint or two. I saw how ye looked at each other this evening."

Elizabeth says, "Nonsense."

"Beg pardon, I recognise that look – God knows but I do."

Elizabeth shakes her head and says, "There is nothing between us."

Hannah says abruptly, "If you're not going to use it…I really need to. There's a gentleman upstairs with a big purse waiting on me."

"You'll die young,' Elizabeth says, "and may you die in a hole, and never find peace there."

"Go to Hell, yourself."

Elizabeth raises her hand but Hannah's face is braced to suggest she's been slapped too often for another to cause her concern.

"You're a filthy woman, McGarry. Dirty and foul and pure evil."

She walks.

Dennis, you fool; swine have more honour…wait until I get my hands on you. You're ruining us in every possible way.

*

The column decamps not long after first daylight. He had not slept well, his night spent tossing and turning in the cloying heat, always a film of sweat on his forehead. Many times he had prayed to God for the will to act in the coming hours, to do the right and honourable thing, whatever that may be. Whenever he thinks of his nephew, his heart fills with unfathomable sorrow – there are moments he feels as though someone has brought a spade to his innards and is digging these out. Images unfurl of the youth as a boy and then on the cusp of manhood. So much potential in him… lost to king, to country.

He wears his best red jacket and white breeches, the black boots polished up by his batman. Dons his three-corner hat with its braided rim. His sword sharpened and scabbard blessed with a drop of oil to speed its release. His flintlock primed.

*

In less than 20 minutes of marching, the rebel encampment comes into view. According to the ordnance map the area is known as *The Long Hill*, an ascending gradient which ends at the ancient rath.

The solid mass of beings disturbs him a little. So many. Perhaps 3,000…though 4,000 might be the closer estimate, in keeping with reconnoitred reports. His steel is tested, he shifts on his saddle to disguise his discomfiture from his fellow officers, to make them think it is merely saddle soreness that prevails and not tints of doubt and fear.

Be still, think. I have a 750 mix of dragoons, yeomanry and militia, well-armed, trained, and already victorious against the insurrectionists. And those bastards are in an attitude of defeat.

As they advance, he orders the dragoons to fan out and the troops to advance with rifles forward, bayonets fixed. Cantering ahead with three delegates he holds up his hand to signal halt and next motions Cannington to meet the rebel walking toward them. He is waving a white flag. Back and forth wildly, stretching the rag because nature is far from eager to do so. The sun is loud on the earth, the grass burnt to rose gold. Skies hold not a trace of a cloud. The heather is purple on the flanks of the Wicklow mountains. Duff rests his eyes there for seconds, then notes the carcasses of dead sheep and thinks how these fellows dined well – had partaken of food not theirs.

On his instructions his company had given wide berth to the expanses of furze from which rebels could have sprung a surprise attack. Even so, he feels that they have not afforded themselves enough space. Yet, he reminds himself, they are here to surrender and to receive protection notices.

I am being overcautious in the extreme.

He brings his eyeglass to his good eye and sees ahead: extinguished campfires, rudimentary implements used to fashion shelters, scattered too are green cockades, bunting, flags with yellow embroidered harps. A tapestry of lost hopes, discarded prospects, defeated ideals. Dejection.

Cannington returns at a slow gallop. He salutes and says, "Sir, the rebels are prepared to surrender in accordance with the terms of the amnesty – Lord Dundas is said to be on his way to oversee the handing over."

"Indeed."

Next, he signals for his company, "Advance!"

Slowly the column moves, closing in pincer movement on the rebels, until separated from them by mere yards. Rising in his stirrups Duff cries, "Pile your weapons where my men indicate and stand yourselves back..."

He watches the weapons loom into a tall and stout pile, hears constantly the rhythmic falling and clashing of steel and wood. Cast on to the heap by sullen men, and by some who consider the whole process a reason for jesting. Through this facade he can smell their distress, notices the fear, anger and bitterness in their faces. Quelled. In need of further quelling.

There is a growing disquiet among them, dark mutterings, as though they are going against the grain of some deep instinct and coming to regret being parted with that which is as much a life preserver as a taker.

With the surrendered weapons heaped high in several areas, he orders the rebels to retreat, the calvary edging forward.

The 180-degree cordon of his men advance, like a tightening noose.

Duff digs his spurs into the flank of his charge, rides beyond the cordon, and shouts, "Get down on your knees the lot of you and kneel for pardon."

Reluctantly the rebels ease to their knees, most on one. Duff hauls air into his lungs, so much it scalds, and the vines in his throat bulge from the haranguing he issues…what he says trickles fury and ripples of realisation into the mass. In the aftermath a strange silence descends – a fear and a great wealth of nervousness, not confined among the rebels, pervades.

Discharging his flintlock Duff roars, 'Spare no rebel!'

The thunder of hooves resembles the drumbeat of thunder. The cordon empties their muskets into the tightly knit throng of rebels. Duff discharges his other flintlock, unsheathes his sabre and runs it through a fellow standing arms outspread, his face blank with shock.

"No quarter!" Duff extols.

But his voice is lost in the cries, screams and shouting. The sky a vivid blue, the mountains to the east stark and rich with flanks covered with heather and trees of varying greens and on the plains the black cloud of massacre, the reek of gunpowder and blood, the blazing of gorse where rebels had sought shelter.

*

'My dear General,

(I have witnessed a melancholy scene). We found the rebels retiring from this town on our arrival armed. We followed them with dragoons. I sent on some of the Yeomen to tell them, on laying down their arms, they should not be hurt. Unfortunately, some of them fired on the troops. From that moment they were attacked on all sides. Nothing could stop the rage of the troops. I believe from two to 300 of the rebels were killed (they intended we are told to lay down their arms to General Dundas). We have three men killed and several wounded. I am too fatigued to enlarge. I have forwarded the mails to Dublin.'

James Duff, General.

*

McGarry put the boy to making a shelter in the depth of the bog – if they are to survive the winter, they will need a dry hideaway. A dwelling that hard rain won't wash to nothingness, or harsh winds tumble. Bogland is a place for a festival of winds to happen, each searching for a true direction The lad is good with his hands; he would cobble something together, though he often has to advise him of the pressing nature of the task: it is not a work to be put on the long-finger – for when snow begins to drop around their ears. What is of use, they will plunder from the derelict homestead, stones, bricks, iron work, stuff like that.

Meanwhile, he intends seeking out William Aylmer of Allen, a well-connected man, a rebel leader who had gone to Dublin and survived the battle of Tara in Meath. He and his men have taken to the bogs too, some miles toward the Lullymore region, according to the old woman from whom he bought some eggs this morning. She added there was a fierce amount of men making their homes on the bogland. Men who had hitherto known only luxury.

"God bless the bog," she had said, "though it's not for the long while that a body ought to linger in its arms. Not fit for a Fitzgerald prince, the bauld heathen Silken Thomas, back in the day…a spoilt pup of a cratur, he was…"

McGarry'd smiled at the toothless and bare-footed woman – her *back in the day* was 1531, and the heathen a noble of Kildare who'd rebelled against Henry VIII, whom he'd wrongly blamed for imprisoning his father in the Tower of London…

He mutters, lad "…not like that, let me show you…see, bed the stakes like it'd take thunder and the power of God to shift."

Carty's response is to do as bidden, when he pauses to draw breath and say, "God doesn't hear us, does He?"

"Indeed he does, He's just not listening."

*

Midnight, before the massacre

En-massed on the long hill, gathered in groups around campfires, or engaged in cooking and cleaning, gathering furze sticks for the fires, the mood within camp switches from broodiness to enrapture at the thoughts of pardon, to broodiness again, back and forth… never an in-between mood of evenness. A coin endlessly pitched and tossed, falling as it wills.

The majority of rebels are generally attired in dun-coloured grey that had originally been brown before washing, mostly fabrics of frieze, corduroy, and off-white shirts. Most have shed the green cloth, not wanting to antagonise the militia. They converse freely about tomorrow, the works in need of doing around their homes, the return to the way things once were – which were better because the days were certain and in the last month they had been far from such. And Father Farrell on his rounds spoke of peace and the bounty it will yield; a sure promise of seeing dawn…he'd suggested it was wise to discard the white bands around their hats, to lose also the green cockades, and the items they'd taken from the military whom they'd killed in battle; for these are as much instruments of war as the pike and musket – and the dragoons and their kind are easily provoked. Hatred is harboured within their hearts…

"Give them no reason to flay the flesh from your bones…the Kilcullen United men have returned to their homes, pardoned, unharmed, and this is what we want too – to reconcile, to put the dreadfulness behind us…for them to stop tormenting us, and for stability to be in our lives."

Every ten minutes there are reports of riders approaching and on each occasion it proves not to be Tiernan with news of Lord Dundas, but instead people who have heard of the amnesty and want also to surrender their arms. They arrive in dribs and drabs, very many of them uncertain if they are doing the right thing but assuage their fears by telling themselves that so many people here present could not be wrong. There is safety in numbers, if one remains with the flock. The talk of the militia merely drunk talk, uttered by very few.

Art O'Byrne is becoming edgier, contagious, and making Dennis so.

What the hell is keeping that man?

Of a sudden a man approaches and says gruffly, "I've a message to deliver to you. Your wife is poorly and you're needed at home."

Dennis glances from O'Byrne to the messenger who shrugs and says, "An oul lad asked me to tell you…it's taken me two hours to find you, so don't go tasking me with sentry duty or heaping questions at me…I've a belly in need of food." Then he is gone to a nearby trestle table, pushing his way between people to claim a slice of black bread.

“You’re not going,” Art says, “do I make myself clear?”

Dennis's look is sharp. He has no doubt there is feck all wrong with Elizabeth; it is something she wants of him without lending any thought to its consequences. Like or lump it, he is an officer until his surrender is accepted and he receives pardon. Still.

“It’s not a long distance,” he says.

A disgruntled O’Byrne turns his back to him and speaks with some other officers, wondering aloud if they should send a rider down the Kilcullen direction to determine what is keeping Boots Tiernan.

“A good idea,” a voice says.

Dennis glimpses his son coming to him – his eyes double check. His heart thumps hard with joy and then faster and harder with concern – he should not be here. That silly, silly woman. Unless. God, he thinks, perhaps there is actually something seriously the matter.

“Jack,” he says, going to him, squatting and taking his upper arms.

“You’ve to come home, Mother said,” Jack whispers, “she got a warning that it is not going to be well with the hand-over.”

“Did she now?” Dennis says suggestion in his tone for Jack not to be unduly concerned – women are given to exaggeration.

Jack nods slowly with uncertainty.

His boy’s arms are thin sticks in his grasp. He pats Jack’s head and says, “You came alone?”

“I left grandfather in a field – he wasn’t able to come this far – well, he was, but I don’t think his heart was in it and he was thinking too of the walk home.”

“There’s nothing ailing your mother, is there – she’s managing those bastards all right?”

“So can we go, now, Father?”

"Son."

"I don't like it here. Why are so many of them drunk? That is not right. Why doesn't Father Michael give out to them?"

"Jack."

"Let's go."

"When it is done with, I can go home – we need the notice – or we will not be left alone – that's how it is – they have us in a bind, Jack. A curse of a bind."

Jack shakes his head, "Mother is right. You never listen. There is going to be no getting of papers tomorrow."

"No redcoat officer is going to risk having us as a huge force roaming the country. It'll make their suppression of us more difficult and long lasting. And these are my men – do you want to have a father as a coward, one who leaves people in the lurch?"

"You have done so with your family."

He slaps the boy hard across the face. Immediately regrets it. Jack stares numbly at him, his eyes welling, aware that people are looking, had noticed a flash of violence happen at a place least expected. Shame fills Dennis.

Jack darts from him, ignoring his father's call to stop. His name, "Jack!" carries huge remorse, but the boy does not care. He wants to be away from here with its reeking smells of tobacco and ale and burnt soup and smoky fires. And a man who does not want to know. Who could be told something 20 times in each ear, see what ought to be done 20 times by his own eyes, and still be intent on going down the wrong way.

For a second he thinks to hurry after his son, but O'Byrne calls him, "Dennis! This may well be Boots."

By the time it is realised that it is not, Jack has long gone.

He consoles himself with the knowledge that by this hour tomorrow, it will all be over and he'd have the notice in his hand.

He could return to Elizabeth knowing his home would not be torched, his family molested, himself without fear of being hung or incarcerated.

Never again would he put himself and his dearest at risk. In addition, he would be able to look men in the eye – they would know that, unlike the likes of McGarry, he did not jilt his oath to the United Irishmen. That he treated an oath with the utmost respect and importance. He would hold fast for the sake of a future.

*

"No sign of Dundas or his overseers," O'Byrne says as the militia drummer begins to beat the arrival of Duff's column from Kildare town west. It is morning, not long after daybreak. Tuesday.

He hands the eyepiece to Dennis. The troops and dragoons are dispersing into a horseshoe formation, leaving a sole route of escape, to the east – but as they draw nearer this avenue too is severed. His spine turns cold as he studies the manoeuvre taking shape. Steady, he tells himself. Steady. He has his horse. He can flee in an instant, keep a tight hauld of those reins.

O'Byrne goes forward, leaves the rath, carrying a white flag. Waving. Turns to beckon the men forward. Their advance is slow, cautious, tinged with apprehension. The day has a mood, darkening.

It is done. The capitulation.

After Dennis hands in his weapons, he re-joins his own unit. He senses no relief among them. A neighbour, Dalton, comments that he sees no tables being set up – on which the notices would be signed. And O'Byrne too makes this observation as he passes Dennis, adding. "In Kilcullen, the men received a notice at the same moment they parted with their weapons."

There isn't time to discuss the discrepancy because General Duff has ridden to the front of his troops. He orders the rebels to kneel for pardon. His tone is harsh and laced with menace. His whole body seems coiled, shoulders raised, his chin high.

After he has listened to few rebels haltingly beg for the King's clemency, he shows intention to part with none; …SPARE NO ONE. The first volley of shots put low a dozen men; the dragoons sally forth, using lances and sabres, trampling men to the ground. Dennis's horse takes a lance in its flank and sinks with him as its knees buckle. He falls from its saddle, lies slightly foggy headed, throbbing head. Around him, he witnesses dreadful carnage and savagery. Unarmed men are slaughtered, some die in the mode of anger attempting to fight back, others run and are cut down amongst tall thistles. Screams, curses uttered, sunlight on sabre blades, gunfire lowering men, shot in the back. Splashes of blood drench his face, shirt, stings his eyes…

He too curses under his breath, for his being a fool. He clears his eyes with his shirt and gets to his feet.

Seeing a narrow space open between cavalry, their riders busy cutting at men, he flees, not daring to look either side of him. He is aware of others running too, of their being cut down. More than half-expects to hear a horse galloping behind him, to feel the thrust of a sword or a ball cleave him. But he is almost close to a belt of furze – he would merge into its midst and crawl to safety – out of view, some way safe, if not entirely, because they would burn him out.

Don't look back.

But he knows well the sounds associated with hunting and looks over his shoulder. Two dragoons have spotted him and are in pursuit. He stumbles, rights his balance, just about. Ahead at least two militia foot soldiers block the way to the furze.

Veering right he approaches a low stone wall – the riders are almost upon him. The sound of hooves commingle with the roars of the dragoons, scalding his heart – there is none of him which is not terrified.

Climbing atop the wall he gathers two hefty stones and hurls one at the first rider, catching him square in the face. The other, he misses. The sabre runs through his shoulder. Expertly, the rider twists the blade before withdrawing, leaving Dennis to crumple and fall to the ground.

Winded, dazed, and losing a lot of blood. In severe pain. Dennis pictures how his blood must be fanning out around him like a red cloak. There is blue in those rebel skies and red soaking into the colour of green.

*

The house is theirs again: suddenly, the troops have gone, gilded for war, leaving a wake of work behind them in the form of cleaning, of ridding the place of their odour. No sign of Brian or Jack and it almost noon. Or Dennis. Has he enlisted into the militia, the feck? she thinks. She wouldn't put anything past him. There is a sour atmosphere at play. It is as though the black shawl draped over her shoulders is preventing any light from touching her.

Of Dennis, she has not made any decision. She will spill Hannah's news and he'll deny it. Leave him? Perhaps. Though it will be difficult to fox her way around this world without a man. If that is what he is, now.

Within the space of an hour she has snapped several times at Sally for little or no reason, for moving too slowly, for leaving a lick of porridge in the pot after saying she'd cleaned it thoroughly, for singing a song while feeding the hens. For fiddling with the quartz teardrop stone she'd plucked from the Crawford's garden. Her childish voice grates on her nerves. This is not her real self. Worry can shift the soul out of a person. She would apologise to the child in a while, when she grows into a mood to listen. Now…

What! Such a commotion…Musket fire…screams, screeches, roaring. Startling her.

Sally comes running, her face drained of colour. Slaughter is happening on The Long Hill.

*

The soldiers are about to hang me, and they laugh at my terror, my flow of urine, breaking of wind and worse. Dismiss my cries, that I should not be hanged; told them who I am. A Reverend.

'You'd say Mass you Popish piece of dog cock.'

It is over for me – I am to them a Catholic priest, in truth it's not my garb they confuse, there is a rage of blood lust in them. A chain, they wrap a cannon chain around my neck to hang me and bludgeon my face and body with their gunstocks. I close my eyes and try to pray, but no prayer falls, because my thoughts are awhirl, and the pain of Christ's suffering is upon me, the tightening, the agony…but a prayer is heard, for I hear my brother-in-law, Simon's roar for them to release me, you imbeciles…harm him and you'll be shot.

The rest, I forget.

*

McGarry spots the riders slow to a halt at the ruined cottage, his attention drawn to them by bird flight rushing high from the bog cotton. Three. On horseback. Dennis? But his squinting eyes reveal it is Boots Tiernan and two others. One heavily bandaged at the shoulder. He gathers they had encountered an enemy patrol. He allows the spiny gorse lapse into place, collapses his scope.

Are they being pursued? he asks himself.

It may be too late, but "Smother the fire," he says to Carty, "quickly."

They are in a small moss covered clearing surrounded by dogwood, thickets of bushes, furze, brambles of blackberry; ringed by tall marsh reeds, and mushy bog.

The men are half a mile distant if you know the path of the bog, two miles if you do not.

Annoyance sweeps through him: why did I take that boyo Boots into my confidence?

Tell him the whereabouts of the family home? To use the place as a marker to wait out my visit. Then, on the other hand, there is some extra safety in numbers, but yes, now, problems too; it devalues the whole idea of hiding low.

"Let's go, and come here till I tell you something about handling this," he says to Ted, "…you sure eyed little bugger."

He moves along the winding trail, avoiding bog-holes, enlarging his step and leaping here and there – a stick to prod a surface of which he is still not too sure. It has been a nightmare with the horses, walking them to the hideout – a stray thought, a wrong stride would bring disaster. A bog slows a man down, slows time.

The way the bog is, because of its nature aligned with his stealth, they do not see him until he stands before them, appearing between alder and hawthorn trees, remaining in their shadow, in front of the foxglove. The men are sitting with their backs to a gable end. Weapons across their legs, within easy reach. They are surprised to see him but try not to reveal it.

I am right. Something is amiss.

He watches as they pick themselves up and proceed toward him, their eyes locked onhis.

"Roger," Boots says, forward of the pair.

A Judas dance?

The wounded man is not injured at all, but is using his bandage to disguise a small pistol. He points it squarely at McGarry's chest.

"Is this what – who are these men?" he says.

"Lord Roden's,' Boots says, "they are for Generals Lake and Duff."

"I see. So they are not men."

"Shush," says the man holding the pistol, bringing it close to McGarry's cheek.

Boots says, with nervous apology, "I had no choice – they would not cut me a letter of pardon unless I gave you up. They caught me as I made for Dundas."

The armed man says to the other, "Seize his weapon."

When motioned to, Roger brings his hands above his head. His flintlock is roughly grasped from his belt and cast aside. The pistol holder, eyes on McGarry, removes his bandage and instructs Boots to use it to tie their prisoner's hands behind his back.

"Quickly."

The shot that rings from the shelter of trees takes away Boots Tiernan's face.

McGarry half-turns to run but is easily wrestled to the ground by the man securing his hands. His compatriot loosens his blunderbuss in the direction of the shot and shouts, "Let's go… leave him, leave him…We don't know how many of them there are!"

The man hesitates – McGarry rolls away, struggles to his feet.

Another shot rips through the bog air.

*

She peaks her hand across her brow, but squints nothing of what is happening on the Curragh Plains. Smoke from the burning furze bushes blot the skyline. After having Sally hide in the cemetery and warning her to stay there until bidden otherwise, she hurries along the road, planning to turn left at Dolan's Field. She hasn't gone much of distance when she runs into a crowd rushing in her direction.

"Go back Missus, go back, Jaysus," a young man says, a rasp in his throat.

"What's the matter?"

A woman answers, "Bad news! Bad news! Our friends were all slaughtered on the Curragh today."

Another voice warns, "Don't go there, Miss! You'll be sliced like a pig."

She is a rock in the middle of a stream of people in a hurry to create a distance between themselves and a dreaded horror.

Move.

But her feet are rooted. Jack...Brian...Dennis. By inhaling and exhaling several deep breathes, she fractionally composes herself. Keeping to the narrow grassy verge, looking at the faces of those passing her by, recognising few, acknowledging no one, she continues her journey. Then she spots her father-in-law hobbling, being helped along by Jack.

Hugging her son, tears falling, she says to Brian, "Did you get word to Dennis?"

The old man averts his gaze. She smells liquor from his breath and pucks his arm, "I told you, didn't I, not to go drinking – what sort of man are you to do that at a time when people need you. And you, Jack..."

"I-"

"Mam, I had to stay with him – he wouldn't wake up for me after I had seen Father," Jack says.

"You saw him?"

"Yes, we spoke."

*

They return home to wait out the time. A soreness and a heaviness in her creates a deep-rooted realisation that something terrible has happened to Dennis. Time is holding back exactly what that is, like a show master waits for his audience to settle, before bringing back the curtains. She can wait, has to, but it does not mean she must sit still.

She sits alone in the front garden, watching the smoke rising from the Curragh grasslands.

The skies freckled with murders of crows, are stains of sin chalked against the blueness of the sky, tainted further by an underbelly of battle smoke masking the devil's handiwork.

She closes her eyes and listens to the drone of the bees on the trellis of honeysuckle, a contraption Dennis had fashioned. Often this summer, before the world went mad, they would sit on the form and smell the scent of the flowers he had just watered and now… Cannington who, slightly injured on the Curragh, had told her that no one would be allowed on to the plains to claim their dead. The General's intention was for their bones to bleach in the sun. Any person caught going there would be hung and his body left along with the rebel corpses, for his bones to likewise bake.

"He means every word," he'd said.

For now, all I can do is watch the cloud of crows above the dreaded sight.

*

On the evening of the massacre, Duff sips at a rare vintage of whiskey. It had been a good day – upon viewing the sum of rebels gathered on the plains he had initially experienced a momentary flight of panic. Fear. But this was replaced with anger and a burning desire for vengeance. They were no more than murdering scum, an ill-educated drunken rabble intent on wreaking mayhem. Freedom? From what? Their drudgeries. They will exist, always – changing your master does not bring a new world order.

They are no less well-off than their contemporaries across the water, and one does not witness those rising up against the authorities. Why not? Because they fear and respect King and Country. This little island will always belong to England, even if by some fickle act of fate, it ever wins its own parliament. *A big brother will always be a big brother.*

He had left a guard on the plains to stand watch over the battlefield. The only bodies taken from it were those of his own men, three – two more had died from their wounds this evening. Five fatalities, in total. Not too severe a tally when measured against those of the rebels, 360 of these lay sweltering on the grasslands. Cannington had reported 85 widows grieving along Claregate Street, the main thoroughfare in town. It would be a memory, he told the young officer, to keep those with insurgent tendencies from further rebellion.

In the end, he relents, orders that the families can claim their fallen traitors.

It is not over.

Wexford County is in turmoil. He expects to be directed there to assist General Lake. But first he has to begin preparations to make for Dublin in a couple of days, leaving behind a small contingent to keep watch – he will issue instructions for no nonsense to be brooked, for the smallest misdemeanour to be dealt with severely.

So yes, they can go picking for pieces, not knowing if they are gathering those that belong to their husbands, sons and daughters. A fitting end. Indeed.

*

Not a solitary word has he spoken to Nellie in several days. There is a temper in Patrick and it's directed at Nellie for being present in front of his very eyes when his daughter is not.

A minimum of civility he pays me.

He forgets her loss, ignores her pain; yes, she had been less than gallant in how she had done nothing to try and save those precious to her. Hiding in the hedgerow, having slinked there like a fox into its lair. Trembling all over, hearing the cries of George and

Louise, the yelps of little Rex, as they speared him to stop him from barking protest at what they were at. God, even a small dog had the courage to try and save them. No one else knows this secret, and she imagines her son's coolness toward her would shade darker if she were to reveal the truth of her actions. Or non-actions.

She looks at the maid, brings her eyes to the door, to leave them alone in the drawing room. Outside a cart rolls by and a man calls out that he has newspapers for sale.

Patrick is sat by the empty fire, sniffling, his legs crossed. Pipe in hand, tin of tobacco on a small table to the armrest, a glass of scotch. Scarf ring and blue scarf beside these, speckled with shaver's blood. Ann Marie is visiting her sister in Blackrock, in whose company she finds some solace. Nellie sits opposite, her hand in the palm of her other on her lap.

She says, "You're the same as me, Patrick, I bore you and you have my cowardice for sure."

His eyebrows join in puzzlement, for he understands she is telling him something and yet is revealing only a little. The lines across his forehead deepen.

Continuing she says, "Indeed, it's certain and true. As much as the temper is in you, I don't see any sign of action on your part. Attending to your shop every day, feeding your ample belly with the best of ham and porter. What happened has not ruined your appetite, I've noticed, nor does it deter you from attending the alehouse too frequently for a man who purports to be a gentleman."

Silence.

"That's something for you to deliberate upon. Why didn't you accompany the militia to avenge your daughter's death, instead of skulking here in your city hedgerow. I'm an old woman – you're supposed to be a man. Don't be venting your anger on me – those long brooding silences of yours are intolerable. Go shift your fat lump and distribute your anger to those more deserving of it."

He scratches his temple, sips at his scotch.

"Patrick! Do you hear me!" Her tone mustered with all the bile within her.

Unfazed, Patrick says. "No one blames you, Mother – I am angry but I'm no soldier. I am like you – what more do you want me to say? Is there a worse thing that I can admit to?

Do please tell."

*

Elizabeth determines not to leave her husband's body on the plains. It is not a Christian practice to sit idly by, nor is it a Christian edict to enforce upon a people in mourning. She has accepted her husband was killed in the fray. And if she fails to act on this fact, yet to be determined as such, what sort is she? She will not linger for time to announce; she will push against the clock. At the very least, doing something will make it appear as though time is moving quicker. That it does not own her.

She goes to Chadwick's House off the town square where an aid post has been set up, bringing some loaves for the wounded soldiers, though her throat has to chew on bile. Elizabeth enters the hall. There is a quietness, with no one about, not even a sentry, though several are poised like hawks outside the gates, blind hawks that hadn't seen her veer to her left. There is a thick odour of disinfectant, a sudden cry, and then silence. The door bursts open and a surgeon is busy talking to someone over his shoulder – they wear butcher's aprons, the bloodstains fresh. They stand, blind to her.

"...you have read on up on a new surgical procedure, you say – and you think it might work in this case."

"Yes," says the young man.

The senior man with the grey moustache the wingspan of a small bird, says, "Tell me, what would you have me do with Cannington's wound – a ball went clean through his thigh."

"I would apply to the wound a dressing about two inches thick and a couple of yards wide. I would steep the band in whiskey and then fasten it to a slight rattan and pass it through the wound, withdrawing the rattan and leaving the bandage in the wound – this will suppurate and heal..."

She takes her chance.

Cannington's ward is a former sitting room and it holds several beds. His is the nearest and she hastens to it. He is groggy, his eyes glassy, his face pain pinched.

"Elizabeth," he says through scummy lips.

"I brought you some bread," she says.

He nods slightly.

“Do you need water,” she asks, while bringing a small pitcher to his lips.

'Why are you here?'

“It's about my husband.”

He listens to what else she says, his eyes half-open.

Weakly, he advises her of what he has heard. Duff’s decree. Its subsequent change.

“He might not be dead,” he says, “but rather could be left there to die.”

“Where do I look, where he is most likely to be found. You would know.”

“No, I don’t…a battlefield is a rough sea…things drift. And the truth of it rarely, if ever, drifts to shore.”

“What am I to make of that?”

“Exercise caution…it’s still a battlefield, still a stormy sea. The sight of it brings a curse to your soul.”

*

A while later she has Henry, an occasional farmhand, fix up a farm cart with a dray horse.

He stands there awkwardly, the sweat thick on his wrinkled brow and his fingers on the rim of his hat, wanting to dissuade her from going to the plains but afraid of rising her temper. His hazel eyes seek out Brian for support but the old man says nothing. Next he shifts himself under Elizabeth’s hard gaze and hands her the reins.

She allows no man to come with them, because she knows that they have already lost too many. Sally comes along and Jack too. They need to see for themselves what the folly of war does to people.

Elizabeth is not alone; there are others making the pilgrimage of salvage.

*

My dearest brother, Charles.

I know that by now you have received my dispatches concerning the brutal death of your poor boy. I am now sitting outside Kildare's sole remaining tavern, drinking whiskey. But this I hasten to add is in celebration at our victory won today.

Some 360 rebels lie dead on the plains and their leader, O'Byrne, is across the road from my table. A prettier sight in death than he was in life, this rebel swine. He does not sway.

Such a lesson he is to the tawdry rebels and the townspeople.

The town itself is quiet, the people too afraid to as much as peer out through the windows. The local population is quartering my troops – the conqueror living at the expense of the vanquished is another reminder of the might of the Crown. I will quarter tonight in a suitable house currently being sought out for me by my officers and then make haste for the capital as soon as possible. I know, Charles, that this news of the rebel decimation is small comfort to you in your loss, but I cherish the notion that at least it might be of some comfort.

Your brother-in-arms, James.

*

The man falls hard at McGarry's feet. His eyes open. He watches the other ride away, in so much of a hurry he is not even properly mounted. McCarthy emerges from behind a sturdy belt of lilac, warily, cautiously, pointing a flintlock.

"Good lad yourself – check the bodies for money – I'll go see to their weapons. Let's get a shift on."

"Do we bury them or what?" Carty says, looking down on Tiernan.

He is on the balls of his feet, flushed and well-pleased with himself.

Tell you this, McGarry thinks, amn't I the bright one for choosing a sharpshooter as my companion?

"We'll feck them into a bog-hole," McGarry says, "we don't have the time for digging graves."

Still, the work is laborious and time consuming, and there is the danger of being seen. It can't be helped. Proper disposal is vital, a sinkhole he knows of, where the ancients buried their sacrifices to their gods.

Back at their hideout, two horses, several weapons and some supplies to the richer,

McGarry comments tiredly, "That was a lucky escape – do you see how you can trust no-one, son, do you?"

"Yes."

"They had some money on them. I think you should take it and get out of here, lad."

"Where would I go?"

"Liverpool. England…who'd look for a body in a graveyard – do you get my meaning – they wouldn't stop to think that a rebel lad would hide among them, yeah?"

"They'll be others that'll come this way, do you think?"

He waves a paper at the young man, "Do you know what this is?"

"No."

"Tiernan's protection notice – you can pretend to be him – it's that for which he sold us out."

"I want to stay."

"Take it anyway," he says, offering it to the young lad, "you might change your mind."

"You should go, Roger. Your face will be too familiar here always, your name too. A danger to yourself and those around you. I will be okay – I am less recognisable than you."

He had not expected to hear such clarity of reasoning from one so young. The lad is right. If he stays, he will never know peace until he is in the grave. He does not push his conviction that Ted is wrong to spurn the opportunity to flee. He is young enough to begin life anew, while his old head isn't. But…I owe this young man my life.

*

She tells the children to wait, never allowing them to get too close to a sight of the dead. Bodies mangled, limbs lying scattered around, eyes missing from their skulls, the birds feasting, cawing mightily when disturbed. No sign of the guard.

Elizabeth loses count of the bodies which she has turned over. Contorted, bloodied and disfigured faces as some are, she recognises them. Despite the handkerchief she had earlier soaked in whiskey and pressed to her nostrils and mouth, she frequently has to break away to retch.

*

The shiver in his bones, the ice in him, the cold of the grave, he thinks. Too weak to crawl any farther, he lies on his side, using a clod of grass to staunch the bleeding. The pain is not too bad, now. He thanks his maker for that small blessing. On several occasions he has opened his eyes to see the birds near to him.

He had seen the riders' hurrying from him to chase others to cut down and by God had he smiled when he saw that some smart boyos had hidden their muskets in the furze. And though one was sabred in the belly, the other loosened both firelocks and brought two dragoons to their deaths, the surviving Suffolk turned and bolted.

He closes his eyes and imagines he is free, running towards home, away from this blood drenched place. Running – and he sees Jack and he is walking the dog. But he doesn't see Elizabeth or Sally. He thinks it a terrible pity that he had ever stopped looking in their direction.

*

Still, there is no sign of him. She thinks that perhaps he had indeed escaped and is in hiding.

Moments ago, she witnessed two women dragging the body of Father Farrell to the edge of the furze and bury him; they scraped the hard earth away in a desperate hurry to be away for fear the militia might return.

No sign…there are more bodies near that fallow field at the end of the slope, by the track that Brian calls 'The Race of Black Pig,' a trail that used to knit the raths to the Fianna's hill fort on Allen. She looks at the wooded hill – she had once visited there with Dennis, bringing Jack to a woman who lived at the bottom of the hill, who cured him of warts. The old woman had warned Dennis to keep himself to himself and his own business.

Funny how an unheeded warning always returns as a ghost to tell you that what happened need not have, that we had been forewarned – we had forgotten the healer's counsel.

Then again, not all of Jack's warts disappeared as she had promised.

Hold…over that low wall with the dislodged stones.

There….

Yes…Jack, Sally! Quickly!

She directs the horse to a nearby gateway, cracks the whip until she is through.

Elizabeth distinguishes him by his britches, their dun colour and the brown jacket she had darned at the side of the elbow. After stopping the cart, she dismounts and hurries to him.

On her knees, at his side, she calls "Dennis!" Her children either side of her, begin to cry.

"Dennis…Dennis!" she says, imploringly.

He is sun warm but long gone from her. She holds him, brushes his curly hair, sweeps her hand over and through it, cradling him and in the cradling she is nursing all their dead dreams and hopes. Next, she slaps his chest; driven by despair.

Jack and Sally attempt to stop her from hurting herself, but her grief is too strong. The women who had tended to the dead priest draw her to her feet. Calm her to a shivering calmness. They lift her husband onto the cart, cover him with hay.

"Let's be away, the lot of us – for if we're seen we could be lying here, too," one says.

*

She drives the dray to Laragh and buries him in a grave that his father had stayed sober enough to dig and lay him therein with a short prayer. He would scatter old dirt over the mound, for the grave had to be put so that it did not look new. For people talk and talk often breaks a neck and she could be searching for Dennis again on the plain. Duff might want to impale the heads of the leaders on the walls…as a warning. Who knows anything now for certain?

*

Nellie is beside herself with joy after hearing the news from Kildare, that the rebels have been soundly thrashed by General Duff and his men. The relief of the city's citizens is quite palpable. She feels in better spirits today because of the news and by the fact that Patrick has begun to address her civilly.

He'd told her that every pot and pan and plate and saucer lost to her would be made new, that the family home would be rebuilt. He has a magistrate's word on it.

The gentry and law people are furious at the barbaric treatment she'd received and if it lay within their power they would gladly return her husband and granddaughter alive to her, also. Such a weight of sympathy…she warns herself not to bask in it.

"There is one thing more, Patrick," she says as he accepts his coat from a maid.

His shoes are gleaming, she notes – he looks polished in himself.

"Mother."

"Our servant girl…"

"Yes?"

"She will be working for the family. If she is alive."

He scoffs, "Hardly be working for you otherwise, Mother." He bites on his lower lip, then says, 'Oh, I'm not sure – not in the least – I doubt very much if Ann Marie would want her around the place."

"We must show we are prepared to move on, to forgive as our Lord forgave. Patrick."

"How very gracious of you," he says, with a touch of underlying sarcasm.

"Leave the running of the household to me – I will do the hiring and the firing – the reprimanding."

"As you wish."

*

Kitchen noises. A pot bubbling. People gathered around a table. A woman's laughter. When he enters the room and takes to a seat reserved for him, he wishes he had stayed in bed. He looks around and speaks to the officer beside him, "This Hannah woman, she's a flighty thing is she not?"

Duff had spoken with Hannah two hours previously, when she was manners and politeness, damning her brother to hell for his activities…saying if she knew where he was she would lead his honour's fine troops to him. Directly.

"Sir, she's a good source of information."

"You would do well to remember that you have a wife worrying about you at home."

Duff thinks how difficult it is to control the lusts and desires of men after a battle in which they had brushed against death. But that woman, more so than others who'd accompanied them here: *her laughter grates on my nerves.*

She forgets too easily this one, talks too much, and has tripped up on the truth a few times by contradicting herself. When corrected she gives a wave of her hand, a giggle, as though a lie is a small thing and the truth an object to be twisted into any shape of her choosing.

"Stew, Sir?" the officer says.

"I will partake, yes."

He needs something to refresh him – he is sorely tired and the morning would be here before they know it. He reminds his command of this and warns them to quell the din and not to have him, "…after I retire, come down from my bedroom."

The time will come when he says this and he'll have to leave his bed to reprimand them – that will signal his retirement from his Majesty's service.

Those present fell silent, and he wonders at his words being king much quicker than usual until he follows their eyes to the door that has been brusquely opened, without knocking.

A woman. Pale-faced. Pretty. She stands with her eyes taking in the scene.

He says, "One should knock before one enters. Did the sentry let you pass?"

"This is my home, gentlemen, and the sentry knows me, for his wife buys my eggs and she owes me for some."

Duff says, "We are free quartered here. Myself for this night and some of my officers thereafter for a period yet to be defined."

"Be careful then in dealing with that which is not yours. Your men have stolen much from me – on several occasions my home, my food…and…"

He admires her courage – but she is like someone who has lost much – a little more would be a strain to her. But there is resilience written all over her.

"I will, they will be careful" he says, "and I am sure you'll be here to tend to the needs of these brave troops."

"I can't say that will be an honour."

Duff says, "Your husband, is he about?"

"He is away on business down the country."

"Tis well for him. I am glad he was not at Gibbet Rath."

"I-"

Duff interjects, "Are you going to stand there in the doorway all night, my good woman?"

Elizabeth steps forward, closes the door behind her.

"This stew is very tasty," Duff says.

A woman's cackle erupts, as though in teasing the General about his lack of taste.

Elizabeth in cold fury says, "Hannah McGarry, shame on you.

Shame. Many good men are dead, men who you knew, and knew overly well, I dare say. You laugh and joke with their killers. Show some respect."

Duff feels compelled to say, "You are distraught about little."

"Little, Sir? No life is little. You are not God."

"I avenged the deaths of good people today. Old men and women and a young officer, killed for no reason by butchers."

"Were the people not provoked into rebelling?"

"Provoked you say? They were preparing for rebellion and if we had not acted and disarmed them of weaponry as much as we had done, then tis the rebels could be sitting here eating your stew – but it seems to me that you would not mind that so much. Away with you, now, while my temper is still even."

Elizabeth turns to leave and then sees a smirk on Hannah's face. She rushes at her and scrapes her fingernails down Hannah's left cheek. A shriek of pain rents the air. The men closest to the scene pull Elizabeth away, but such is the determination and ferocity of the attack that it takes them a minute to haul her outside.

Duff believes that the woman has done some good – she's quietened the women in their company into an uneasy silence, reminding them that there is a reckoning. Always, a reckoning.

*

A new life. He has taken the boat not to England but to America, working his passage in tandem with partial fare to pay his way– and his mood is low as it has ever been. He understands he has no choice other than to become a ghost. He watches the gulls, spits into the white quake of sea, then looks at the land for as long as the vision holds and then curses it silently under his breath. Prays for his friend at home, a rebel, alone on the bog, Roger.

*

He had not expected to be feted like so in Dublin. It is a splendid occasion. Over high tea, he briefs his superior officers on the events of the previous days and earlier. There is mild reproach from one of the English officers, Lord Rothschild, who questions the severity of the treatment meted out to the Curragh rebels. This takes him back somewhat.

He says, "My good Sir, I doubt very much if Lord Dundas were to ride into Dublin that he would receive so great a welcome for his leniency towards the rebels."

"Be that as it may, General. But by offering such generous terms Lord Dundas has brought much of that area into our control and it is now peaceful."

"They need to know our wrath in order to discourage them from ever contemplating rebellion again. Let us not be soft on an issue that requires us to act like soldiers in defence of an honourable realm."

Lord Rothschild is a wiry man with high cheekbones and a broad forehead, punctuated with a strawberry birthmark that he touches as he says, "Soft, is it? Your actions revealed your lack of formal military training – regarding strategic purpose."

A voice cuts in.

Duff believes it might have been Lake, but his eyes are so fixed on Lord Rothchild's he cannot discern.

"Please gentlemen! We have other matters to consider. Wexford is in open revolt and we have lost several large towns there."

He cannot resist saying, "Offer them lenient terms!"

This time he knows it is General Lake's voice, 'General Duff! Well done, you.'

*

Elizabeth worries at the silence of her children. In the last few days they have become pale and gaunt. And become anxious and nervous when anyone speaks to them. Although most of the troops have since moved to Wexford; she has five living in her home. Ruffians, eating their food as though the supply is endless, careless with their furniture – undoing all the years of the minding of these heirlooms. Insulting them at every opportunity – they themselves reside in the barn, entering their home only to clean up after the pigs and to prepare their meals.

She hands Jack a tankard of sour milk and a thick slice of barley bread which he devours.

This is it, Dennis, your legacy, bringing the force of these hard hearts upon us. When one of the soldiers found the flintlock, you'd hidden in a metal box on the top of a shelf in our bedroom, he waved it about and created such a fuss.

It was easy for her to say she knew nothing about it because it was true. How could she have known – the top shelf was way beyond her height. It was her husband's space. His only. Now he is no more.

*

At the ball held in his honour he is with people who think as he does, who welcome a hero. When the musicians break he notices an elderly woman smiling his way, and who appears anxious to speak with him. He excuses his fellow officers and approaches her.

Nellie says, 'I have been so wanting to speak with you all evening, General Duff.'

"I'm here, now, Madam."

"My name is Nellie Crawford."

She is aware that her name would mean something to him. Earlier in the evening, she had had Patrick make him aware of her losses.

"I've heard of the dreadful circumstances, Ma'am, and you have my entire sympathy."

"I want to personally thank you for avenging the deaths of my husband and my poor granddaughter."

Pride surges within him. Words like these break the boulders of small doubts.

"Thanks are not necessary; I merely did my duty – my only wish is that I was not in town earlier to avert the atrocity and others."

"You are not God and so weren't to know, General."

"You're the second woman within the space of three days to tell me that I am not God."

"Ah, but perhaps you are his hand."

"Yes… I pray so," he says.

"Is it safe for me to return to Kildare?"

"Safer there for you now than before."

Silence.

He says, "You will return?"

"Oh yes. If I stay away, it would be giving the rebels what they wanted. My son and his wife are coming with me. Their decision has bolstered mine."

"Splendid. I will give you a letter to hand my captain and he will ensure your safety, if needs must by placing a guard outside your home, but this you will find is unnecessary, for the cracked whip is still ringing in their ears and the town has been got rid of its treacherous souls."

"There is a favour I would want to ask of you, but first I must explain myself and my reasons."

He listens intently and reflects for seconds before saying, "I see. This is what we will do."

*

Elizabeth had spoken with some women today, widows like herself. And was told that a procession of widows live on one street; as we own a black plague road, *The Road of the Corpses,* leading from the Friary, now we have a place of widows.

A total of 356 men are believed butchered and more are expected to die from their wounds. The militia let them live on account of their suffering being great.

She'd seen one of Roden's Foxhunters today, too. He was talking aloud to his officer about the fellow who had thrown the stone at him and left him ruined. He said he was in great pain, Sir…ladened with a pair of crutches. I won't be able to ride to Bunclody. My apologies for it. The bastard who got me is dead – I found out after that his name was Dooney. Downey, Elizabeth had thought. Dooney and not Downey. She walked on by, bringing her shawl around to cover her face, to hide the forming tears and the anger that if she did not bridle, would see her as dead as this so-called Mr Dooney.

*

Nellie received a sum of money in advance of the compensation due, presented to her speedily as the authorities were keen to see people such as herself return to their home places. She thought her Patrick was kind to have organised the replacement of windows and doors prior to their arrival. The rebels had not set fire to the house but only because a man called Roger McGarry had had designs on it.

When he first entered the house…Patrick said there was blood on the carpet and the imprint of a child's hand on the wall in blood. It fair took him a while to have it cleaned: he did so in complete rage and sorrow.

Though they are well set up with this new arrangement, some doubts are visiting her: if they are doing the right thing by living in a home where their loved ones perished, among people who saw and had hand and act in seeing them perish? Ann Marie seems to suffer inner convulsions at the prospect.

*

She makes up her mind to sell the farm and move away. There is a 30-year lease on the land, because no Catholic could hold a title longer than that span, and the price is fair, as there remains 20 years on the deeds. Brian had agreed it was a good idea.

Often she sees Dennis in her dreams, always smiling to begin with and then his lips close tightly like he would do whenever someone has vexed him, or he is that way toward himself.

*

Those first few nights back in her bedroom she used hear the noise of the front door breaking open, hear the windows smash, hear the cries of George and Louise and she had to bite hard on the edge of her blanket so as not to cry out.

The nightmares less in intensity and frequency; the first time back in the house after, after…it haunted her during the day, still. She could not enter the house on the day of her return. She had to coax her heart along. She stood and stared at the open door – the hallway appeared a mile long. Sweeping her courage into one corner of her soul, she walked in. Saying she wanted these curtains changed and this and that done and talking loudly and incessantly till she was left alone. Then…alone…she cried.

*

Elizabeth had spoken with her friend Jennifer Smith and felt envious toward her, and found herself becoming irritated. She said that her John and a man named Talbot from Kildare town were earliest arrivals at the Rath and surrendered their pikes. They retained two fire pieces which they had hidden in the furze less a half mile distant from the Rath. Having handed in their pikes the two men began to set off. They didn't mind handing in their weapons, but they were not going to bow down to the king. In the meanwhile, two cavalrymen were sent after them: Blackhorse or Suffolk was the regiment she mentioned. Hearing what was going on behind them they fled.

One of the pursued, Talbot, was wounded by a sabre thrust. Talbot's companion, her John, shot the two soldiers, then after concealing themselves he staunched his friend's wounds with yellow clay and later brought him home.

Jennifer wanted him out of there, but John said no and so they hid him under a trapdoor in the bedroom. He died after a night spent in awful pain. She had had no troops being quartered in her home – God is either with you or against, Elizabeth thought, wishing her to leave her be, to take her cheery self away. Husband and home intact…*what did I do to deserve the opposite?*

*

Oh, the brazenness of her to come knocking on my door. I knew she would, though, now fully knowing her kind.

Their ways.

Patrick's friend from his university days in Trinity, a quaker indeed, Abraham Shackleton, told him of the Ballitore parish priest who'd pleaded for the life of a prisoner whom the rebels later shot – Patrick recalled, his memory strong and lasting, '…Abe said the priest appeared all day of wavering counsels, sometimes before them, persuading the people to surrender, and other times apart, haranguing them to opposite measures.'

Nellie had tsked and aired, "He would turn on a sixpence, like a dog George brought home, one side of his face brown, the other white. You had to look at the creature head on to see both his colours."

Their ways.

Nellie purviews her former maid with an artic eye. A mild morn, no breeze. Passive skies, but there is an autumnal hint, and she loves the autumn. George had too. It was their favourite time of the year. The withering as opposed to the ripening. Strange, Perhaps. But they loved the changing colours of the leaves, the falling of chestnuts, the coolness of a river walk, the picking of berries, a scent of sap bleeding from trees – the lead into winter and bitterly cold winds, heavy snowfall, ice…the windows draped with frost…the fires constantly burning…wishing for the ripening of Christmas…But this woman in front of me cheated me out of seasons with my loved ones, stole their lives…the treasures of tomorrow.

She buries a ton of hatred, umbrellas it with a fawning smile to hide her feelings.

Nods at her visitor, who'd the audacity to knock on her back door, which her man had answered, and left her standing there until he reported "…she says she is Hannah, Ma'am."

"Hannah, what is it?" Her tone even.

"Oh Jay Mistress, it's awful since you've been gone and when I heard of what happened to Mister Crawford and little Louise, sure I wanted to die myself and they dressed me up in your clothes and did terrible things to me and I don't think any of us will ever be right in ourselves again, sure how could we be?"

"Hmm, Hannah – you were kept as a prisoner."

"Yes,' lowering her head, "I was hoping you might be of mind to forgive me…I felt so ashamed of my uselessness to you in your hour of need…but I did call, I did, but you had left."

"You poor thing. Indeed, Hannah, I'm aware that you called."

Pauses.

In her next breath Nellie tells her she can start the morrow and in the afternoon she finds where Captain Cannington is quartered and has her man ready the hansom cab, telling no one of her business.

She pauses outside the gate then opens and closes it behind her. She would always have an issue to do with crossing thresholds – since her's was so cruelly crossed – she has wakes of the mind.

Her presence startles Elizabeth as she turns the gable end carrying a basket of washing for the clothesline.

"Mrs Crawford!"

"Mrs Downey."

"I did not expect to see you again."

"Many did not, I dare say. Many hoped not."

"Well I for one am glad that you have come home."

"Hmm."

"If I can help you in any way, to clean, to…"

I will tell not this woman who I have come to see. Cannington must be elsewhere – there are no troops here. I can tell.

"Your husband. The cart he lent me to bring Louise to Dublin, it was damaged. I will reimburse him for his loss, tell him, as soon as my full compensation arrives."

"Compensation?"

"For the destruction of property, the cost of two funerals and so forth."

"We are all after having lives lost and property destroyed."

Silence.

"Yes, well, to the victor the spoils, is this not the case, always?"

"Is there anything else I can help you with?"

Brazen it, Nellie thinks, go with it, "I wish to speak with some of the officers. Are they here? A Captain Cannington perhaps?"

Elizabeth advises her of the infirmary's location. They would know of his whereabouts.

*

The price Elizabeth fetches for the farm allows her to buy a much smaller property enough of a distance from Kildare. She wants, needs to shield her eyes from the sight of the place. One of the militia officers bought it, having taken a bit of a fancy to its layout – *a fancy to me, too, I dare say;* tis bad enough they killed my husband without wanting to take his place in our bed.

*

She hands the letter to the officer with the bad limp and he reads it twice over and then does as detail in the letter instructs; to burn it in front of her eyes.

Cannington says, his features set hard, "It'll be done. Of course."

He continues, "You heard your granddaughter call out this woman's name."

"I heard."

*

The following day is Hannah's first back at work and she has worked hard. Perhaps done as much in one day as she would have done in a week in her previous spell with us, Nellie thinks.

When Hannah is about to retire for the evening, to make for her cottage lodgings in the street of widows, Nellie gives her extra chores. It annoys her to stay on late but her words if not her expression are pleasant about it.

"Unless you are much too fatigued to continue, Hannah – are you?"

"Only it'll be dark, Ma'am, and I do dread the dark since…"

"I see. Your lodgings are not miles remote from here."

Reluctant, still.

Nellie's dark frown persuade a change, "I am tired Ma'am, but I know there is much needs doing and so I will set to it forthwith."

"Good. After that you'll make tea and heat the scones that cook baked; I'm sure Patrick and Ann Marie would like those for supper, too."

"Ma'am."

"Strawberry conserve."

"Ma'am."

"Then you can wash, wax and shine the floor from threshold to kitchen. It can never be clean enough, I think. No matter how the floor shines, there's always a shabby appearance to it – at least in my eyes. It's rather a large hall, I know."

Silence.

"You will, of course, be compensated."

"Oh there's no need for that, Ma'am."

Polite, civil and respectful to each other, as they have always been.

Near midnight, Nellie says she can go home and she cheers her a little by presenting her with a green bonnet, seeing as she loves them and they bring up her smile so well. Tuppence in her pocket for her extra time. How well she looks setting off, Nellie thinks. Such a lovely smile.

Patrick and Ann Marie gape at her when she informs them of her actions. Scone crumbs rest on their plates, tea drank to the base of their China teacups. Her own scones left untouched, her tea cold.

"Mother?"

"We need to hire a new maid, Patrick, one of the black women Ann Marie spoke highly of in Dublin, yes…we will not be hiring any more local help."

*

There, there.. matters did not turn so badly after all, Hannah tells herself, as she approaches the town well.

*

The day before departure for their new home, she walks to the Curragh. She had been of half a mind for Jack and Sally to accompany her but decided against. One would not imagine to look at the rath and plains that it was ever layered with mutilated corpses. Stands of thistles here and there, the mountains distinct, and the Hill of Allen too. The shine has gone from the furze.

Along the trail of the Black Pig she walks to where she had found Dennis. The grass is warm to the touch of her fingertips. Here is the last place she'd felt the warmth in him…here…he had torn the future from his family, for unreasonable and selfish reasons.

*

A week later her family come looking for her. Nellie exclaims surprise that she had failed to turn up for work, that she felt very badly let down. And when you do eventually locate her, she says, "…tell her that her job has finished here. I had to take on new help in her stead."

Astonished they are. Hurt, too – for employment is so scarce.

Patrick later breaks the news to her about the military sealing the well, for its water has turned bad and is making people ill.

He says, "How did you know the water was bad, and to stop us drinking water taken from it?"

"Call it a woman's intuition."

"The locals, though, they sipped."

"I said nothing to them. I thought it was okay for them to drink what they were used to."

"I see," he says, beginning to understand.

Nellie says, "God love them. A new well is needed."

"Isn't all just a splendid new start?" he says.

"Isn't it just – it is all just," Nellie says.

*

1808, a cabin by Killinthomas Woods, near Rathangan, 12 miles from the Curragh.

Elizabeth thought, *It is the decade of remembrance.*

Among few there exists an escutcheon of pretence, as though no one wishes to own their truth; it's best to keep it quiet as a lonely whisper in the corridor of their hearts, so others may not overhear the bad things done in the name of rebellion – they shroud their souls, not to veil their guilt – of which there is little or none – but so as not to be caught and face the magistrate, or for someone to exact retribution for the killing of their family member. Blood may dry, be washed away, but its spilling is never forgotten, will never dry on a clothesline no matter how strong the sun or the airy and drying breeze.

For many it was not for freedom they fought but instead were driven by disaffection with their daily lot. Our daily lot was what we returned to, without those who had at least made enduring it tolerable. Streets rich with widows, labourers shorn from the fields, fields of daisies grown by the bodies of croppies, young men who'd fleeced their skulls of hair lest the yeomen tarred and pitched them – these days some haunt the back corners of churches, face blotched with wine stains, flesh pitted by the searing tar, broken spirited yet seething with hatred. Corked for now, for my generation, till the bottle breaks once more.

Occasionally I miss being with Dennis, miss his teasing half smile, his saying I was taking too much sugar with my tea, that it was not good for my teeth, citing Rotten Tooth Kelly's brownish stumps. That diabolical summer ten years ago, my God, the speed of time.

This summer is wet, black clouds frequently threaten, and winds rise wantonly and bring my imagination to think they are the sighing of the dead, of wandering souls in want of their lives back to live over. A chance to breath again, to touch, to know love, loss, and indeed, pain. Back then the sun burned and the ground hardened, and 1000's died, more of us than them. A great and terrible culling.

The memories…

A grand turf fire burns, and a wood log is a goodly sparkler. The glow is of the morning sun…

Our son is not the same since that Curragh day, for days Jack bled tears from his heart, he shook and trembled, shed weight, his pallor turned and has remained alabaster – he resembles his father except he's leaner, more hidden, his eyes can't hold others, always ready to swipe to the sides, and this trait draws attention to him. He is akin to a miser rarely opening his purse so people can't catch a glimpse of what he holds inside.

He worries and disturbs me, so much so often that I can't sleep at night. Our little mud cabin is cold in winter and hot in summer, my bed chamber is small, but comfortable with my last good possession, a decent feather bed. Jack minds the fencible sword his father had taken from a dead captain in the yeomanry. He treasures it as though it were gold. His eyes, I believe their softness, the normality of holding those of another person, faded with the dying of a summer sun upon a field drenched in blood.

Dennis – I remember more nowadays that I could in the early days of my loss.

Betimes images come fresh as freshly squeezed milk. Small detail like those in a landscape painting in a lord's manor; you never have enough time to dwell upon – but the eye steals for your mind, and they latch like a barnacle to the heart's hull…the sight of our son wide-eyed upon his father's gashed body; Dennis stretched on his back, his knee raised, his face bloodied from deep cuts, dust from the earth stuffed into his mouth – steeped in blood about his chest, his ear severed…his eyes open, meeting his son's…and an image, a fox who'd been nibbling at the dead, which we had chased from my husband, on his haunches at the edge of gorse, patiently waiting for us to go…It's Dennis's dead eyes that haunt our son, I think. The rigid stare fixed on the skies, as though a dream has gone out of sight. It's the blade Jack sharpens and polishes, the freshly painted handguard, that makes me want to throw up; he has his father's eyes. And we own still the dream of a cause – or a curse.

If the rebel vidette had not left his post, he or they could have warned the men of Duff's aggressive intent, his flanking manoeuvre, the cannon, but he had taken flight with the bauld McGarry during the night, thus abandoning his dawn and forenoon watch. But that night, I'm told, every caution was thrown as wet peat on a dead fire – no mounted sentinels remained at post. All believed the deal was done, sealed and signed, about to be delivered, as what had occurred with the Kilcullen army, none of whom resurrected their pikes and banners in protest at the massacre of their fellow wearers of the green cockades. Instead they remained mute and cocooned in their homes, clutching their letters of protection, thanking God it wasn't them. Cowards, self-tethered…it is small wonder the winds come to bemoan and berate.

Jack, I breathe his name, watching him cross the fields to the meeting point on the wooded hill, walking at though it is merely an idle exercise on a drizzly day, wildfowling for a pheasant, snaring for a rabbit. The land encircling the woods is owned by a catholic loyal to the realm during the rebellion, but is not now, since the war, his stomach churned by the slaughter of his kind, I believe it's said of him. But his loyalty to the king did not save his businesses from failing in the aftermath of '98. One would almost feel sorry for him. Almost.

If I thought Jack would listen, I would push him hard to leave the country, as I had done with Sally, who works as a maid and cook in Cardiff, to be safe, to clear the fog from her future, a role vested in her by Nellie Crawford, who has since passed, God bless her. Passed on the stairs upon which her husband had perished. I would warn him as I told his father, that a throw of pebbles never broke the gable end of a stubborn wall.

What escapes me is why he engages with his father's lost cause, given his condemnations of Dennis for his dereliction of duty and care to his family. Surely my diatribes on the same matter would have strengthened his resolve to steer clear of rebellion.

There is only hope found in prayer, that I am not alive to see another breakage of glass.

Epilogue

Excerpt from *Bone Deep*, short story, published and anthologised by The Stinging Fly, published in *The Mango War and stories*, New Island, translated into Danish. Winning entry in the Inaugural Cecil D Lewis Literary Prize.

*

They found a woman's skeleton in a well at the market square. The well had been covered by a grey boulder I used to sit on while waiting for a bus to turn the corner at the traffic lights.

The council had moved in with bulldozers and donkey-jacketed men to put a new face with new EU money on an old landmark. But for that reason the skeleton would not have been discovered.

A TV expert suggested the skeleton was over a hundred years more, probably more.

Experts never give precise answers to anything. They hedge their bets and in that way can never be totally wrong – never being wrong is extremely important to a lot of people.

Especially experts. My father is an expert.

He said, because he is an expert in local history, that the skeleton probably fell into the well during the ructions of 1798 and could *well* be an ancestor of ours.

A McGarry, eh? he joked, of all things.

Most likely, agreed my sister Hannah.

Acknowledgements

A partial list…to those who encouraged me along the lonely road, my deepest appreciations and gratitude… Ciaran Carty, Seamus Hosey, Dr John B Keane, Mr & Mrs Joe Malone Snr, Dr Mike Collins, Jamie O'Neill, Noel Buckley, Sean Judge, Seamus Boyle Solicitor, Jo Calam, Brian Dobson, Brian Byrne, Gaye Shortland, Tim Binding, Kildare Arts Service, Arts Council of Ireland, Margaret Galvin, Conleth Hill, Pam Brighton, Aidan Mathews, Barbara Sheridan, John Whelan, Richard Ford, Michael Longley, Deirdre Madden, Military Police NCO'S Mess and Military Police Association, Ann Enright, Colm Tóibín, Conor El Sabia, Dan Bolger, Deirdre Nolan, Deirdre O'Keeffe, Eoin Purcell, Anthony Glavin(Margaret Galvin, Phil Nolan, Sean Nolan, Shea Tompkins, Ireland's Own), Gerry Mulrooney, Breda Parker, Mrs P, Philip McDermott, Faith O'Grady, Jim Brady, Alan Dukes, Enda Kenny, Pat Kehoe and more – not forgetting my wife, Valerie, who knows how to fix things that I had thought irreparable,

www.ingramcontent.com/pod-product-compliance
Lightning Source LLC
LaVergne TN
LVHW030921080826
845145LV00013B/3004

* 9 7 8 1 0 3 6 9 2 4 6 1 4 *